Jill Jarnow

BANTAM BOOKS
TORONTO • NEW YORK • LONDON • SYDNEY • AUCKLAND

RL 6, IL age 11 and up

A SHOT AT LOVE

A Bantam Book / February 1985

Cover photo by Pat Hill

ISBN 0-553-24386-1

Published simultaneously in the United States and Canada

PRINTED IN THE UNITED STATES OF AMERICA

O 0 9 8 7 6 5 4 3 2 1

A Shot at Love

Chapter One

It was one evening in early December, and my family and I were all at the dinner table. Mom, Dad, and my little brother, Greg, were all happily munching on their roast beef when I spoke up. I was in a bad mood, and I guess I was taking things out on my family; my tone of voice was pretty grumpy. "You know, the Potters are going to Florida for Christmas, and Barbara Lane's family is going to California," I complained. "How come Dad's the only one who gets to go places in this house?"

I'd sort of brought the subject up out of nowhere, so everyone looked at me, surprised, but nobody said a word. "Do you realize," I continued, "that I'm sixteen years old and I've never even been on a plane? At this rate, they're going to be obsolete before I get to go anywhere."

My mother responded first; she sounded annoyed. "Samantha Jane Alexander, we've been over this a million times. Dad travels so much for Globex that the best vacation for him is just being home with us."

Then Dad spoke up. "But I can appreciate how Samantha must feel," he said in between bites of roast beef. "It does seem kind of a shame that you and the kids never leave North Hollow while I crisscross the ocean several times a year. I'll see what I can do about it."

The weeks went by, and Dad went off to a camera convention in Frankfurt. By January I had forgotten the whole thing. Dad, it seemed, had not. Good old Dad. At dinner one night he broke the news to us.

"Everything's set," he announced. "And you, my dear children, are going to be very pleased. Not only are you getting your first plane ride, but you'll be getting a trip to paradise, too."

"In February, during your winter break, we'll all be flying to Saint Martin in the Caribbean for a seven-day stay at the Paradise Bay Hotel," explained Dad.

"Is Paradise Bay one of those gigantic resorts with a movie theater and a swimming pool?" Greg asked excitedly.

"Absolutely," confirmed Dad. "It has nine tennis courts and some of the most gorgeous beaches in the world."

"It will probably be eighty degrees while we're there," added Mom. "So we'll really be getting away from winter."

"What do you think, Samantha?" Dad asked, a smile spreading across his face.

"Paradise Bay," I said and gave a big sigh. "It sounds heavenly." I closed my eyes, picturing the white sand beaches.

It was easy to imagine what we'd all do. My parents, of course, would spend the whole vacation on the tennis court. Mom is a great player, and she always makes a fantastic impression on anyone who watches her. Small and slim, with brown, shoulder-length hair, she bounds across a court in her neat, white outfit like a real pro. Dad isn't nearly so good. He's tall and thin, but his movements are slower and a little awkward. As usual, he would insist on wearing his white tennis hat, which is three sizes too small for him, over his short, graying, blond hair while he tried to return Mom's volleys. Greg, who is a skinny, short, freckle-faced nine-year-old, would probably spend the whole trip playing human cannonball in the pool or plugging quarters into video games. To me, paradise meant lounging around the pool, working on my tan.

I look a lot like Mom. I'm a little taller than she is, but we're both thin and muscular. And we both get really dark in the sun, while Dad and Greg just get red blotches. Mom and I get the same red highlights in our hair from the sun. At that time my hair was my pride and joy. Dark and silky, it hung below my waist. Paradise Bay was going to be a real beauty treatment for me, I thought. My skin would turn golden, my hair would turn reddish, both of which would make my eyes appear greener.

"So, Samantha," Dad asked, breaking into my reverie, "does this qualify as going away someplace special?"

"Does it ever! Dad, you're the greatest! And winter break is almost here, just"—I counted fast in my head—"seven weeks away. How did you ever think of going to the Caribbean?"

"Let me explain. You know all the times I've hosted regional Globex Camera get-togethers for employees. There was one in Chicago last August and one in Los Angeles in October."

"Like the one we all attended in Montauk a couple of summers ago?" I asked, memories of a very unpleasant, very private incident popping into my mind.

"Right," confirmed Dad. "We have these get-togethers periodically to help promote the idea of family at Globex. We feel it's good for business. So this year we're all taking our families to the Caribbean."

"Oh, great!" chimed in Greg. "That Montauk trip was neat. We got to meet a lot of great kids, like Jeremy and Keith Garson. Boy, I'd sure like to see them again."

"You will, Greg. The Garsons will be one of the other families from the Eastern Seaboard offices taking the trip with us. Instead of a one- or two-day thing, we decided to extend our get-together and make it something really special. It'll be a mixture of business and pleasure, and I'm sure we'll all enjoy it."

I groaned inwardly. "Oh, yeah," Greg said teasingly, "I bet Sam's going to be real glad to see Keith Garson."

"Shut up," I hissed as quietly as I could and still have him feel the force of my threat. Greg had an amazing memory for embarrassing details.

But Mom and Dad were too busy talking about all the details of the trip to notice us, for which I was thankful.

It was a relief to get away from the dinner table to the privacy of my room that night. I needed time to think calmly. Dad's vacation plans would have been fabulous if it weren't for one little problem that could wreck the whole thing for me!

Although I hadn't thought about it for ages, I had done something horrible at that Montauk get-together. Thinking about it, I locked my bedroom door and dug my diary out of its hiding place between my mattress and box spring. It was a five-year diary—its pages edged with gold, and its cover locked with a delicate silver clasp. I pulled the tiny silver key from a secret spot in my bottom drawer. With a busybody like Greg around, I could never be too careful.

Unlocking the clasp, I turned to the beginning of the diary. I knew that awful Globex trip had happened sometime in August just after I was fourteen. I had just gotten the diary.

It was one of those things you wish you had

never done, and once you had, you would do anything to forget it. I opened my book and began reading.

August 10

Dear Diary,

We drove in the station wagon out to Montauk for an overnight stay at the Seaview Inn with a lot of families from Dad's company. We spent the day on the beach and went swimming in the ocean.

There was a guy there named Keith who was kind of a creep. Even though we're about the same age, he's a little shorter and on the pudgy side. He has a mouth full of braces, a fuzzy upper lip, and a voice that cracks. He does have nice, wavy blond hair, though. I looked at it a lot because I was too embarrassed to look at his face.

I tried not to talk to him too much, but he stuck to me like glue. It was gross. I couldn't stand having him around me all the time. He kept offering to get me food from the refreshment table. Finally I said yes, and when he disappeared into the crowd, I got this brilliant idea. As quickly as I could, I ran back to our room. I felt a little weird about what I did, but I was glad I had brought along a good book to read while I hid out there.

August 11, Sunday night

Dear Diary,

Am I happy to be home. Dad's Globex party turned out to be a trip into Guilt City. Last night while I was hiding out in the room reading, Keith Garson had the nerve to knock on our door. He called out my name, but I really was not in the mood to deal with him, so I sat very still and pretended I wasn't there. Later, when Greg came in for the night, he told me Keith was looking everywhere for me.

I started to feel real bad about what I had done, and I decided it would be a good idea to apologize to Keith. But this morning when I went down for breakfast, the Garsons had already left for home. Now I'm just relieved that I'll never have to see Keith again.

Snapping the diary shut, I sat on my bed feeling miserable. Keith Garson was going to be at Paradise Bay. And Greg was sure to say something obnoxious about our trip to Montauk. At that moment I couldn't imagine anything more embarrassing.

So, for the next two days I walked around trying to think of ways to get out of going on our dream vacation. But it was all just a fantasy, I knew. There was no way out. I'd have to go and face Keith Garson again. It was then that real disaster hit. I was helping out with the scenery for a school play. I was sitting on the floor of the school auditorium, sanding some old furniture when Tony Land dripped red paint on my head as he stood beside me painting flats.

It was an accident, I know. He certainly didn't mean to do it, and I tried to look on the bright side. After all, the paint had missed my eyes. It had only gotten in my hair, my beautiful, straight hair that reached past my waist.

When I got home from school that day, my hair was a gooey mess. Mom and I tried everything to get the paint out. I washed my hair with three different shampoos and even tried a special solvent meant for use on hair. Nothing worked.

"Samantha," Mom said finally, "I have two suggestions. Either we can find the best haircutter in New York City to trim it into some beautiful, exotic short style, or"—she took a deep breath—"you can wear a paper bag over your head." Her eyes and mine were both filled with tears.

After all, she was talking about my silky, chestnut-colored hair that had never been trimmed more than half an inch in my life. It was the one thing about me that made me feel different and special.

So she booked an appointment with the famous Mr. Sandro at Kenneth's hair salon, and I cried while he snipped away at my hair until it barely covered the tips of my ears.

Of course, *he* thought it looked gorgeous, and Mom said it showed off the oval shape of my face and my big green eyes. Dad said I looked darling. Even Greg liked it and said short hair was really in. But that was easy for them to say. It wasn't their hair. I didn't care that other kids were wearing their hair short; I wanted to hide until mine grew back. Somehow, when I lost my hair, I lost my self-confidence. Mom bought me some nice new clothes for the trip, but all I was really interested in was a pair of sunglasses and a big hat.

I got so depressed I cried whenever I wrote in my diary.

So when the time came for us to board the plane for Saint Martin, not only did I feel crummy about seeing Keith again, I hated the way I looked, too. Still, I couldn't help being a little excited about the trip. Dad had showed us brochures of the resort—pristine white buildings surrounded by flowers, palm trees, and iridescent blue-green water. It really was like a dreamland.

Dad said that some of the other families, including the Garsons, who live in White Plains, a suburb of New York City, had taken an earlier plane, so I didn't need to worry about seeing Keith on the flight. I thought about him, though, and I promised myself that on this trip I would be as pleasant to him as possible and act in a more mature way. Sitting in my padded airplane seat, with the engines humming, I was able to convince myself that it was going to be just that easy.

The flight took about three hours from New York, and when the plane began to bank for its landing, I got my first glimpse of Saint Martin. I was delighted. It was as stunningly beautiful as Dad had said it would be. The water was as smooth as glass and a hundred different shades of turquoise. Red-roofed cottages dotted the mossy hills and pastures. But most thrilling of all were the long strips of glistening white sand that ran along the edges of the island. It was so gorgeous and so completely different from anything I had ever seen before that I could hardly believe it was real.

The plane touched down on the runway with a kind of bumping that made me clutch the edge of my seat, but my first breath of warm Saint Martin air a few minutes later more than made up for any momentary discomfort. At home, in North Hollow, the temperature had been thirty-two degrees with the threat of snow. In Saint Martin it was eighty-three degrees, and there was a refreshing breeze blowing and a clear sky.

Suddenly nothing else seemed important, not even seeing creepy Keith Garson. I was on a tropical island, and I was going to have a fabulous vacation!

Chapter Two

The airport was a mob scene, but I was too excited by the sensation of an early summer to let all the noise and confusion bother me.

An airport official directed us to line up with our passports for immigration clearance. There were so many people ahead of us, it looked as if we would spend our entire vacation waiting in that line.

You can imagine my surprise when it took a mere twelve minutes for us to reach the checkpoint, have our papers stamped by a man in khaki bermuda shorts, and be released into the confusion of the airport's main room.

The cinder-block terminal was about the size of two gymnasiums. The back wall was filled with tiny souvenir, liquor, and jewelry shops. In the middle of the space were all the airline counters, and next to them was a circling conveyor belt filled with luggage. Mom, Greg, and I stood impatiently waiting for ours to come by while Dad made a quick call to the Paradise Bay Hotel.

It was fun to study the people around us. Wearing brightly colored clothes and lugging suitcases, they looked more relaxed and happier than they would have back home. You could tell the people who were leaving the island by their rich, golden tans. We new arrivals looked pale and sickly in comparison. I wondered where everyone had come from and where they were going.

As I let my eyes wander from group to group, I spotted a guy standing on top of a wooden booth marked with the name of one of the airlines. With a camera pressed to his face, he was clicking off shots of the airport mob scene while precariously balancing on the tiny, slanted roof. I was sure he was going to fall off and break his neck. Tall and lean, with an attractive, athletic build, he was dressed in khaki-colored jeans and a red alligator-type shirt. I watched him, fascinated. How did the busy airport look to him from the top of that booth? I also wondered what his face looked like behind his camera. I waited, hoping to get a glimpse of him.

My patience was soon rewarded. The boy finished his shots and moved the camera down, revealing what looked, from a distance, like an adorable face and a head of soft, blond waves. This guy was cute, cuter than anyone I had ever seen at North Hollow High.

That's when my imagination began to take off. I fantasized that romance was about to come to Samantha Jane Alexander. This gutsy photographer was really an employee of the Paradise Bay Hotel, and I was about to become his assistant, helping him with the job of photographing all the guests. I didn't even know if there was such a job, but it was fun to pretend.

Suddenly I had a great urge to ask Dad to show me how to use a good thirty-five-millimeter camera. He had been offering to teach me for years, but I had never been interested in anything more than the easy-tooperate, automatic cameras. The others seemed too complicated.

"Sam, there are our bags," Greg said, breaking into my daydream and jabbing me in the ribs.

"Greg, would you mind not poking me," I snarled, annoyed that he was interrupting my fantasy. But with one quick look I could see our bags moving away from us on the conveyor belt. Greg and I ran over to the belt, reached through the crowd, and retrieved the two heavy suitcases. Mom had gotten the smaller ones. We also had to grab Dad's big trunk, which was filled with Globex cameras. I groaned as Greg and I wrestled the heavy box off the conveyor belt together. When I looked back for my dream photographer, he had already disappeared.

The ride to Paradise Bay in the hotel van was stunning. A number of the other guests had crowded into the vehicle with us, and everyone was amazed at the view outside the windows. The drive would have been perfect if I hadn't allowed a few twinges of nervousness about seeing Keith Garson to creep into my mind. But looking out the window, I became absorbed in the panorama of green fields divided by stone fences and dotted with tiny gingerbread houses and grazing goats. As the van turned a corner, we got a breathtaking view of the Caribbean Sea, translucent blue-green water surrounding a strip of pure white sand.

As the van turned off the narrow asphalt road onto an even narrower one, we entered into yet another kind of world. Not the simple, ungroomed beauty we had just passed through, this was a vision of luxury. On each side of the road were acres of manicured green lawn and even rows of majestic palm trees. In another moment the Paradise Bay Hotel came into sight.

The main building stood proudly in front of a number of smaller houses, each with a weathered wooden sun porch. All were built of the same glistening white stucco with red-tiled roofs. Brightly colored flowers were everywhere, planted in the ground and in huge terra cotta pots. Tiled walkways led toward gardens and beaches.

"Wow, what a place," Greg gasped in the seat next to mine, echoing my thoughts exactly. Paradise Bay was even more impressive than the pictures in the brochure had been. It was incredible to think that we were going to stay there for a whole week.

One of the hotel's hostesses came out of the main building as the van pulled to a stop. "Hi, we're the Alexanders," Dad said, getting out of the van and stretching his legs.

The dark-skinned woman introduced herself in a musical French accent. "Welcome to Paradise Bay. I'm Martina. We've been expecting you. Let me show you your cottage."

Everyone got out of the van that then took off to deliver our luggage and that of the other guests to the rooms. More hosts and hostesses came out of the main building to help the rest of the families find their cottages. We walked along the tiled path as Martina told us about the facilities. The main building held the dining room, gift shop, lounge, movie theater, and game room. She pointed out the walkways that led to the flower gardens, tennis courts, pools, and beaches.

It was a short walk to our cottage, but the resort was so well planned that our rooms felt secluded and private, set away from the other buildings.

We had two large, octagonal rooms adjoining each other, one for Mom and Dad, one for me and Greg. Each was furnished with beds and comfortable couches, chairs, and desks made of wicker. The chairs and couches were upholstered in cheerful yellow fabric. The floors were made of the same terra cotta brick as the paths outside. The windows opened onto views of the beautiful grounds rather than the other cottages in our cluster.

Now, I don't want to seem ungrateful or anything, but it wasn't until that very moment that I was struck with a horrendous realization. Greg and I were going to be sharing a room for the next seven days and nights. Don't get me wrong, it's not that I mind sharing. It's not that I can't stand a little snoring every now and then. But my brother is the biggest busybody in the world. How was I ever going to have any peace or privacy?

The first thing I did was to change into a rainbow-striped sun dress, which I pulled out of my suitcase. It felt fantastic to be wearing a summer dress instead of layers of sweaters and coats. I was ready in an instant because I didn't have to spend time combing my hair. There wasn't much to get messed up, possibly the only good thing about having short hair. Then I unpacked. Greg had just tossed all his stuff into an open drawer and was bouncing around the room. Mom knocked on the door that connected our rooms and came in. "The welcome party is at five o'clock," she said, standing in the open doorway. "It's four-fifteen now, and I just wanted to remind you how important it is to Dad that we're all there to help him out. I'm going over to see what I can do." She, too, had changed into a pretty, summery dress.

"Where exactly is the party?" I asked.

"In the Buccaneer Room at the back of the main building. Here's a map of the resort so you won't get lost." She handed me a brightly colored sheet of paper. "See you in forty-five minutes," she said as she left.

"Well, I'm going to check this place out," announced Greg as Mom's footsteps faded away. "Especially the game room. I hope they've got Dragon's Lair."

"If you want a piece of friendly advice," I offered, "I suggest you go easy on the video games. You know how Mom and Dad feel about them. If they find you there first thing, they're likely to make it off limits like they did last summer."

Greg considered that fact for a moment. "How about checking out the rest of the place with me, instead, like the beach or the pool? Maybe we'll even run into the Garsons or something."

"Um," I said uncertainly, but I sure couldn't tell Greg that the Garsons were the last people I wanted to see. He'd tease me mercilessly the whole vacation.

I followed my brother around the hotel grounds, past clusters of other cottages, past the pools, the tennis courts, and a path that led to the beach. But each new turn in the tiled path filled me with dread. Was Keith Garson waiting around the next corner?

When Greg finally led me into the main building at a quarter to five, I felt like a person heading for execution. "Want to check out the game room for just the tiniest second?" whispered Greg.

"Sure, why not." I shrugged. It was one way to postpone the inevitable meeting with Keith. As we walked through the white stucco corridors, we stopped to look at a display of glossy color photographs of the hotel grounds. "If we weren't here to see it in person, I would never believe these colors were real," I commented.

"This place is really great," agreed Greg.

There was a little card under one of the pictures: Photographs by Paul Bostwick. He must be that adorable guy at the airport, I decided, slipping easily into my favorite new daydream. My thoughts of Keith drifted away. Wouldn't it be excellent if Paul Bostwick were working here at the hotel! I had never seen anyone whom I wanted to meet more!

Chapter Three

In a few minutes we joined Mom and Dad at the door of the Buccaneer Room. After sticking some name tags on our chests, we began shaking hands with a lot of strangers, all Globex Camera employees and dealers. I must have said hello to about fifty people before anybody under the age of thirty walked in.

First there was a family with a boy and a girl about eight and ten years old. Greg was delighted. Then a family arrived with a girl about my age. She was a lot taller than I, with a cute face and medium-length, black, tightly curled hair. Her name was Meryl Taylor, and her friendly smile was what impressed me most.

"Hi, where are you from?" she asked easily.

"North Hollow, Long Island."

"Really? I'm from Westport, Connecticut."

"On a clear day we can see Westport," I told her.

"I'll have to wave next time," she said, joking.

Meryl was sixteen, and as it turned out, our birthdays were two days apart.

"Do you ever take pictures?" she asked curiously.

"Hardly ever," I confessed.

"Me, neither," she whispered, and we both began to giggle. "It's always seemed so boring," she went on.

"I know what you mean," I agreed. "But lately I've been thinking maybe there's really something in it." Since seeing that gorgeous photographer at the airport, photography had taken on new meaning for me. But this wasn't the time to explain why to Meryl. "Maybe I'll get Dad to give me some pointers while we're here."

"Well, I'm going to work on getting a great

tan. Boy, will my friends be envious," Meryl said.

"I want to get a tan, too," I said. "My other project is to make my hair grow." I described my accident with the paint.

"That must have been awful," she sympathized. She studied me carefully, "But, you know, I can hardly imagine you with long hair. In fact, I wish I could get my hair to look like yours. All mine wants to do is curl."

"Excuse me, Samantha," called Dad. "I'd like to introduce you to a few more fellow vacationers."

"Feeling social?" I asked Meryl, tilting my head in the direction of the family that had just arrived. There were three younger kids and a tall, blond girl about our age. She had a good figure and straight blond hair that went halfway down her back. I was jealous.

Dad introduced Meryl and me to the Vale family, who were from Montclair, New Jersey. Candace, it turned out, was seventeen. Dressed in her lime green blouse and navy wraparound skirt, printed with whales, she was pretty, in a preppy sort of way. Meryl and I, feeling good about our immediate friendship, flashed her our biggest smiles, but all we got in return was a cold, appraising stare. "Hi," she drawled in a nasal voice.

Candace didn't seem too anxious to strike up a conversation, so after a few moments, Meryl and I slipped off through the crowd. "Talk about friendly. Who does she think she is?" whispered Meryl.

"Miss All-American Preppie," I told her, and we giggled.

"Do you have any idea who else is coming?" asked Meryl. "Are there going to be any more kids our age? I sure hope there's someone Miss Sugar Candy will lower herself to speak to. Otherwise, she's going to be awfully lonely."

"There's one guy that I know of," I confessed. "I met him a few summers ago at another Globex thing. I guess he's about our age."

"Oh, yeah? What's he like?"

"Kind of a creep. Candace is more than welcome to him. Actually, I think he kind of had a crush on me, and I was pretty mean to him. I've felt bad about it ever since, so I'm determined to be nice to him this time." It was hard to talk about, but Meryl seemed to understand.

"Do you have a boyfriend at home?" she asked.

"Not right now. I used to, though. What about you?"

"No. But there's this guy I really like."

We talked for a while about Meryl's crush, and then I heard my father's voice. "Samantha, come say hello to the Garsons."

"Oh, gross," I whispered to Meryl, keeping my head down. "How about coming with me? I don't think I can get through this alone."

"How creepy can this guy be?" she whispered back.

"You'll see," I assured her.

But when we stepped through the crowd and I saw the Garsons, I had a really big shock. "Samantha," Dad said, "you probably remember Mr. and Mrs. Garson and Keith and Jeremy. Though truthfully, boys, you've both shot up so, I'd have trouble recognizing you."

Dad, I thought to myself, *that's the understatement of the year.* Although I flashed them all a broad smile, my blood was bubbling in my ears, and I felt as if a tidal wave had just washed over me. Standing in front of me was not a short, pudgy, fuzzy Keith Garson, but a tall, thin, blond guy in khaki jeans and a red alligator shirt, with a camera dangling around his neck. Keith Garson was my fantasy photographer.

"Hi, Samantha," he greeted me. "It's good to see you." Even his cracking voice now sounded deep and mellow.

"Yeah," I agreed, wondering if he were being sarcastic. With my ridiculous haircut and my heavy guilt trip, I didn't think it would be good to see me at all.

"Aren't you going to introduce me?" urged Meryl, and I could tell by her tone of voice that she thought I must be a little crazy.

"Oh, yes. I'm sorry. Everybody, this is Meryl, Mr. and Mrs. Garson, Jeremy, Keith." It was his last name that was so hard to pronounce, and it was even harder to look straight at him.

Meryl and the Garsons exchanged greetings, and I was saved from having to say anything more by the arrival of yet another family, who had twin boys. They were from Waterbury, Connecticut, and they were sixteen. Jim and Tom Randolph were their names, and although they didn't have the same gorgeous, Luke Skywalker looks as Keith, they were cute, with dark, curly hair.

I looked around at the group of strangers, all of whom I'd be spending the next seven days with. It felt sort of like the first day of school.

Except for Meryl, I couldn't imagine what I would say to any of them. What, I wondered, did I have in common with Jim, Tom, or even Candace? As for Keith, well, that was a different problem all together. Stealing glances at him, I felt like such a fool that I wanted to run to my room and hide under the covers. I had thought I had it all worked out. Keith Garson was creepy, but I was going to be his friend, anyway. I wasn't going to like him, but I was going to be nice to him. Now I was embarrassed beyond words. How could I know he'd grow up into such a gorgeous guy?

Through my confusing thoughts and the buzzing of the crowd, I heard my father's loud, public-speaker's voice. "May I have everyone's attention, please," he called, his arms raised. Gradually the room grew quiet. "I have a special announcement to make, which should add a little extra spice to our already delicious visit," he said. "We all know that Globex makes the most exciting cameras in the world." He paused for everyone to cheer. "And I'm sure a lot of you, being Globex people, have become skillful photographers. Well, here's your chance to show off. We're having a Paradise Bay photography contest. Pictures can be either color or black and white, they just have to be taken on this trip. Submit your favorite prints to our main office on Lexington Avenue. Five pictures will be chosen to receive hundred-dollar cash awards, and one will be chosen for the five-hundred-dollar grand prize. All the entries will be displayed in our office gallery. For those of you who have more photographers in your family than cameras, I have brought along a few extras, which may be borrowed. If there are any problems or questions, please feel free to let me know. Meantime, welcome to Paradise Bay."

When Dad was finished talking, everyone applauded, then returned to their conversations.

"Wouldn't it be nice to win five hundred dollars," said Meryl.

"I wouldn't sneeze at a hundred," I answered. "Do you know how many hours of baby-sitting that is?"

"So what are we going to do about it?"

"Start taking pictures."

"Well, someone has to show me how to load the camera first," she said seriously.

"Yeah, me, too," I confessed. "I doubt I could take a prize-winning picture with an Instamatic."

"I wonder who's going to enter?" she wondered. "Keith Garson, that's for sure. Maybe Tom and Jim, too, but they don't really look like photography types, do they?"

"No," I said, "though I'm not sure what a photography type is exactly."

"Well, in my school everyone in the photography club seems awfully serious, if you know what I mean. Keith Garson is the first photographer I've seen who looks like he's having fun. Maybe he's just pretending to take pictures," she added, grinning.

"I've got news for you," I said quietly. "He does not look like the Keith Garson I met two and a half years ago. I'm in shock over the change in him." I glanced over to where Keith was talking to the Randolph twins. Candace Vale, I noticed, had joined their group. "I wonder how Candace does with a camera," I muttered.

"She's probably an ace," said Meryl. "I haven't seen her crack a smile."

"You know, I think I'll learn photography just to prove I can do it," I said slowly.

"Forget it," Meryl said. "I can already tell you're not the type."

After the welcome party, we all gathered in the dining room for dinner. The room was enormous, with high ceilings and huge picture windows that looked onto the sea. The tables were decorated with fresh flowers and tall red candles. The food was delicious, but I couldn't concentrate on it too much. I was too busy trying to find the Garson family. Meryl and her parents were a few tables away, and we had made plans to meet after dinner, but the Garsons were nowhere to be seen. When I couldn't spot them by the middle of the meal, I gave up looking.

"Dad, how come you never mentioned the photography contest?" I asked suddenly.

"I didn't think you'd be interested, Samantha."

"I think it would be fun to enter."

"I'm glad to hear it, but please understand that photography is something to be taken seriously."

"Are you saying I'll never be able to win a prize?" I asked.

"No, not exactly."

"Well, I'll say it then," piped up Greg. "Sam, you'll never win a prize in this contest."

"Gregory!" I cried.

"Children," Mom said, a warning not to argue in her voice.

"Well, Samantha," said Dad, "just remember that a lot of people on this trip are already quite accomplished."

"Are you the judge?" I asked.

"Heavens, no. The judging will be done at the office by professionals."

"Fine, then there's no problem," I concluded. "But I was planning to use something a little better than our automatic camera. When can you give me a lesson with your camera?"

"That," he said slowly, "is a problem. I've loaned it to someone. And I haven't got any other camera for you."

"What! But you said at the reception that you brought along extras."

"That's right," he agreed. "I brought along ten thirty-five millimeter cameras, and at the reception I got eighteen requests, which is why I loaned someone mine. People are going to have to share, and you'll have to wait your turn."

"Bill, I can't believe you can't come up with something for your own daughter," Mom said.

"Hmm," answered Dad thoughtfully. "Maybe there is something I can do at that. Has anyone seen Keith Garson this evening?"

"They're all the way in the corner, over

there," said Greg, pointing. *How did he find them*? I wondered.

"Fine. I'll be right back. I've got a hunch about how to work out this little snag." Dad got up and headed toward the Garson table.

Chapter Four

Five minutes later Dad was back. "It's all set," he announced, sounding very pleased with himself. "Keith Garson is going to lend you one of his cameras."

"What?" I gasped. "But why can't I have one that belongs to the company? What if something happens to it? I'd feel awful." I'd already messed things up enough with Keith. How could I borrow one of his expensive cameras?

"Nothing will happen if you're careful."

"But I don't even know how to use it."

"That's OK. Keith has offered to teach you the basics. And actually, if you want to be a prize-winning photographer, Keith is the right teacher. He does his own developing and printing, and he's already won several awards for his work."

"But . . ." my voice trailed off. I'd never be able to explain. It wasn't that I didn't want to learn photography from Keith. I was just so embarrassed about how rude I had been back in Montauk that I was terrified by the thought of being alone with him. Suppose he said something about the last time we met? How could I ever apologize without looking like a fool? Since there was nothing more I could say to Dad without telling him about that incident, I just opened my mouth and stuffed in the chocolate eclair that the waiter had just put in front of me.

After dinner Meryl and I met as planned and I immediately told her what had happened.

"Great!" she concluded. "Maybe you'll win a prize."

"What about you?" I asked. "If Keith can teach me, why can't he teach you?"

"Well," she said, hedging, "I know we were joking about photography this afternoon, but the truth is that cameras terrify me. All those numbers and dials look awfully confusing."

"OK," I said. "Actually, I was just trying to

get a little company so I wouldn't have to be alone with Keith." It was a painful confession.

"Why, in heavens name?"

"That tall, gorgeous blond is what terrifies me," I explained. "Especially since I was nasty to him when he used to be short and dumpy."

"Oh, Samantha," said Meryl, laughing, "he probably doesn't even remember. Don't make so much out of it."

"I know you think I'm crazy, but I'm sure Keith Garson thought I was cute back then. I acted like I had it all over him. But look at me now with my shaved head. The joke's on me. Ha-ha." I made no attempt to hide my sarcasm.

"Come on, Samantha, things can't be as bad as you think," encouraged Meryl. "He wouldn't offer to teach you about cameras if he didn't want to get to know you. And your haircut looks adorable. So just relax. Now I heard Jim and Tom talking about Splashes, the hotel's dance club. Want to check it out?" It was easy to see that what Meryl really wanted to check out was the twins, so I agreed to forget my problem for the moment. We found a map of the resort and headed off for Splashes. The club was decorated with brightly dyed fish netting, and there were some fantastic lighting effects. It featured a really good band that played both original music and top forty songs.

"Where do you want to sit?" I yelled to Meryl, who was scanning the room through the blinking lights.

"Over there," she pointed out. "I see Jim and Tom in the corner."

I followed along behind her and soon discovered that Jim and Tom had been joined by Keith and Candace. They were all sitting together at a round wood table. "Hi," said the three boys with welcoming smiles as we neared the table. Candace just nodded.

"Want to join us?" yelled one of the twins, and he pulled over two chairs. "It's a little hard to talk in here," he added. "Would you like a Coke or something?" They all had tall glasses in front of them.

"No, thanks," Meryl and I yelled in unison.

We sat around the table and watched a few couples dancing. I was wondering whether any of our group would have the nerve to dance when suddenly the music ended and one of the band members announced that they would take a ten-minute break. A dance record came on the sound system, but it wasn't nearly so loud as the band had been.

I looked over at the twins. I wished they were still wearing their name tags because they looked so confusingly alike. Yet, already, I could see that one was more outgoing than the other. "So, what do you think? Isn't this place great?" asked the more talkative twin.

"I love it," said Meryl, and I knew then that this was the twin for her.

"So who's going to enter the photography contest?" asked the same twin. "Jim and I took photography in school, but neither of us was especially good at it. We'd rather play football, right, Jim?" He gave his brother a knowing smile.

"I don't think I'll be entering," said Meryl. "I'm not much interested in cameras."

"Yeah, I know what you mean," said Tom. "It's easy to get bored with them when all you hear from your father is cameras, cameras, cameras."

"Well, I'm certainly planning to enter," spoke up Keith in his rich, pleasant voice. "Photography is definitely my thing."

"I just adore guys who are into photography," Candace said sweetly. "And, Keith, I'm sure I could help you win the contest. With my complexion, I do photograph very well." Meryl and I looked at each other and rolled our eyes, enjoying our secret communication. Keith had the good taste to say nothing.

"What about you?" asked Tom. "Are you into photography?"

"Well," I started, "I, uh—"

"Yes, she is," said Keith quickly. "But since Mr. Alexander felt obligated to lend out all his equipment, I'm going to be lending her a camera of mine. He had no idea he'd have so many requests."

I flashed Keith a smile of thanks and felt relieved that he had given such a quick and easy explanation. I was feeling so unsure of myself, I probably would have said the wrong thing.

When the band returned from their break, they started to play a fast number. "Oh, I just bet you're a great dancer," Candace said to Keith. "How about it?" She took his arm and led him onto the floor, moving to the beat of the music as she went. Tom asked Meryl to dance, and Jim asked me. I could see that he was really shy, but once we started to dance, he loosened up.

As we danced I managed to steal glances at Keith and Candace. Keith looked as if he was concentrating on the music. Candace was wearing a satisfied smile.

For some reason, I couldn't stand watching them together, though I knew I had no right to be jealous. After all, I was the one who had been rude and insulting two years ago. My feelings of guilt had come back, and I couldn't get them out of my mind. Now, watching Candace with Keith, I felt even more unhappy. How I wished I were the one dancing with him!

Finally the song was over, and we all headed back to the table. Breathless, we all agreed that it was time for something cold to drink. The waiter brought us sodas, and Tom tried to organize a volleyball game for the next morning.

"Volleyball, really, Tom, that's too boring," scoffed Candace. "Can't you think of some better way to spend your time?"

"There's always snorkel lessons or aerobic dancing," I told her. "And I think there's even some guy from the National Football League who's giving a lecture."

"All right!" responded the twins together. "That's for us," said Tom.

"And a famous Chinese chef is giving lessons," I continued.

"Now that's what I'd go for," said Keith.

"You're kidding," drawled Candace.

"Actually, I'm quite serious," he assured her. "I love to cook."

"Don't worry, Candace," I told her. "There's a swimsuit fashion show scheduled, too."

"Uh-oh, I wouldn't want to miss that, either," volunteered Tom. "I hope I don't have a scheduling conflict." We were all laughing when the band finished its second fast number and broke into something slow.

"Samantha," Keith touched my arm, "would you like to dance?" Startled, I looked into his handsome face.

"Sure," I answered. "I love this song."

He led me out onto the dance floor and took me lightly in his arms as the music swirled around us. He smelled delicious and danced even better. Being so near to him felt incredible. I fought to keep from trembling.

"By the way," I said, trying to be nonchalant, "thanks for being so quick back at the table about the photography." I wanted to say just the right thing.

"No problem. Let's just say I know how hard it can be to admit to strangers that you're a beginner at something."

"You figured right," I said. "And I really appreciate it."

"When do you want your first lesson?"

"As soon as possible, I guess," I answered hesitantly. I knew it wasn't going to be easy, and I was scared. After all, it was one thing to talk about learning photography, but quite another thing to actually do it.

"How about tomorrow morning before breakfast? Are you an early riser?"

"For sure."

"Then let's meet at eight o'clock by the lap pool. We'll have our first lesson and make it to breakfast by eight-thirty."

"Sounds great. Thanks a lot." I tried my hardest to sound relaxed, but every word I uttered seemed forced.

The song soon ended, and we went back to the table. Tom and Meryl jumped up and ran to the middle of the floor, and Jim asked me to dance again. Soon Keith and Candace got up, too. I smiled at Jim as best I could, but all I really wanted was for the music to end. I was beginning to feel as if I'd been awake for a week straight. When the song was finally over, I told the others I was calling it quits for the night, and I quickly left.

I didn't have any trouble finding our cottage. When I let myself in, Greg was already asleep, but the lamp on the table was still lit. Either my little brother was being thoughtful or Mom had asked him to leave the light on so I wouldn't stumble in the dark. Although I was exhausted, I was still anxious to record the day's events in my diary—especially since I had to leave early the next morning for my photography date with Keith.

I took the little silver key from its hiding place in my jewelry bag and the diary from the bottom drawer of the wicker bureau. Greg moved suddenly in bed, which made me uneasy. I didn't like to think he knew about my diary, so to be on the safe side, I got up and locked myself in the bathroom.

There was so much to say that I wrote more than two pages.

Looking over my entry when I had finished, I sighed happily. Despite all my worrying, everything was working out really well. I'd made friends with Meryl, picked up a new interest in photography, and Keith—the new, gorgeous Keith—seemed to have forgotten all about my rudeness at Montauk. *Don't count on that,* I warned myself sternly as I shut and locked my diary. *Tomorrow you have to be alone with him, and then you'll really find out just what Keith Garson thinks of you!*

Chapter Five

It wasn't one of my more restful nights. I kept waking up every hour or so to see whether it was seven o'clock yet. By six I was so exhausted that I was too worried to go back to sleep for fear I'd nap until noon. So I crawled out of bed and crept into the bathroom to wash up.

Next I thought about what I should wear for my lesson with Keith. Somehow, I still couldn't imagine that I was going to be alone in an elegant Caribbean resort with this devastating stranger. It was so romantic. But then, he wasn't really a stranger, was he?

I put on my favorite black bathing suit, a one-piece with a very low back, then put white shorts and a red cotton shirt over it. I added leather sandals and a gold necklace around my neck. When I looked at myself in the mirror, I decided the outfit was simple yet sophisticated, just right for a fancy beach resort.

When I arrived at the lap pool, Keith was there already, sitting on a deck chair and checking his camera. "Hello, Samantha," he greeted me.

I gave him a weak response, trying desperately to think of something brilliant to say. "Looks like a good day for photography," I observed. "Not a cloud in the sky."

"Actually, for a beginner, all this light and shadow could be a problem, but a lot can be corrected with film speed, filters, developing, stuff like that." His voice was friendly, but very much like that of a teacher.

"Oh," I answered, feeling dumb.

"But let's not worry about that for the moment," he went on. "I've brought a camera that's pretty easy to use. It'll make a lot of the exposure decisions automatically, and later on, if you really get into it, you can switch to a more difficult one. Have you done any photography before?" he asked.

"Not very much, really. I've never been interested. I always thought of it as not mine, if you know what I mean." Tom had said it the night before, and I knew it made sense.

He looked up at me very seriously. "I do know what you mean," he assured me. "Doing something your family's involved in really takes its toll."

From the way he said it, I knew he wasn't just being polite. I had a feeling he was talking about something that had affected him deeply.

"It's funny," I continued. "Our house is filled with cameras, and I've hardly touched one. Once or twice I've used the Instamatic at a birthday party or something, but it does absolutely everything itself, focus, winding. It practically even loads itself with that automatic cartridge."

"Those cameras can be a lot of fun, but you can't do too much with them. And really it's not that hard to learn to use something more advanced," Keith said, smiling. "Look, the first step is to open the back and thread the film through these sprockets, like this." Sitting on two deck chairs, we huddled over the camera while he demonstrated. "We'll use this roll for practice, so take your time until we get it right." Removing the film and shutting the camera, he handed me both. "Now you try."

Uh-oh, I thought to myself. But Keith patiently talked me through the loading process step by step. He was so clear with his instructions, there was no way I could make a mistake.

"Good," he congratulated me when I finished threading the film correctly. "Now you can close the camera and wind the film into position."

"Easy for you to say." Then I laughed, marveling at his patience and self-assurance. I was beginning to feel grateful to Keith. My father would never have been so calm and clear if he had been my instructor. He would have gotten annoyed that I didn't know what I was doing.

Keith described the workings of the camera's internal light meter, and I gave him my full attention. "This camera has a lot of safety features that are especially good for a beginner," he told me. "For instance, once you take a picture, it locks until you advance it to the next frame."

"So, no double exposures," I concluded.

"Right," he said. "Of course, once you become experienced, you might not like that so much. You can get some interesting effects with double exposures."

"Well, for the time being, it sounds good to me."

Keith talked on and on about how to use the camera, and it took every ounce of concentration I could muster to understand what he was saying.

"How in the world am I going to remember all this!" I exclaimed finally. I was becoming so overwhelmed with the important information that I didn't know whether to laugh or cry.

"Maybe I've told you more than you need to know," he said, almost to himself. "Why don't we walk around and shoot some pictures together so I can tell you a little something about lenses. I've got a bagful here."

I was careful not to groan out loud, but let me tell you, I couldn't imagine what more there could possibly be to say about photography. Was this Keith Garson's way of getting back at me? If he was trying to scare me, he had certainly succeeded.

I walked slowly around the pool clicking off shots. I was feeling awkward and self-conscious, but Keith encouraged me to keep going. "But it seems like such a waste of film," I objected.

"If you're taking snapshots as a reminder of your Caribbean vacation, then I'd say you're right. You certainly wouldn't want three different exposures of the hotel pool. But if you're learning to take good pictures, you have to work harder."

"In what way? Taking pictures doesn't seem very hard, really. All you need to do is push the button."

Keith took a deep breath. "Maybe we should talk about the 'why' of photography before we go any further with the actual 'how,' " he answered.

"That sounds good," I said, trying to show with my smile that I really did care about what he was saying.

"Well, I guess I should know exactly what it is you want to learn from me. If you just want to learn to take snapshots, I've told you just about everything you need to know. If you want to learn about photography, that's another thing altogether."

We sat down on the huge lounge chairs, each of us cradling a camera. The sun was climbing higher in the sky, and the flow of people walking past told me it was time for breakfast. I ran my nails nervously over the bumpy texture of the camera as Keith and I confronted each other. I certainly hoped he didn't think I was being rude again.

"I assume you take photographs, not snapshots," I said.

"Yes."

"Why?" I asked.

Keith took another deep breath and thought for a moment. Was I dense? I wondered. Was the answer so simple I was going to be embarrassed? But Keith smiled. "That's a hard question to answer in one sentence. You've turned the tables neatly on me, Samantha. Now I'm the one who's a little confused."

"I wasn't trying to be rude or stupid or anything," I blurted out quickly. "I don't know a thing about photography except that I could look at certain pictures forever and that others are just kind of boring. Yesterday when I saw you taking pictures in the airport, I was totally—uh—fascinated."

"So you saw me standing up on that booth." He grinned. "It took me the whole morning to get permission from the airport officials. I finally used Dad's Globex ID to impress them."

"But why in the world would you want to do it?"

"Another hard question. Maybe I'll be able to answer you tomorrow when I get my contact sheets back. If the pictures say something about the feeling of the airport, about the people who are traveling, I'll have succeeded."

"And if not?" I asked, wondering what contact sheets were, but afraid to ask.

"I'll have to try again, though I doubt those airport people will let me in a second time. How about giving me a chance to answer your questions tomorrow morning?"

"I'd like that, Keith," I said sincerely.

"Then for now, I call this lesson officially finished. Until tomorrow I suggest you spend time looking through the camera and shooting several pictures of each subject. When you choose what to photograph, remember that you're using black-and-white film."

"But this place is so full of color," I said, disappointment ringing in my voice. I guess I had imagined myself taking dramatic, colorful pictures.

"Ah, but anyone can take beautiful snapshots with color film. With black and white you have to learn to take solid, meaningful photographs."

"I think it's past time for breakfast," I said, getting up from my chair.

"OK, then I guess I'll see you tomorrow, same time and place. Right now I'm going for a swim," he told me, and not only did he not extend an invitation to me, I thought I detected a hint of relief in his voice.

He took off toward the beach, and I walked slowly toward the dining room, looking for likely subjects to photograph. But it was hard to concentrate on what I was doing. It was the teacher rather than the lesson that was strongest in my mind. Was he always this serious? I wondered. I didn't know seriousness could be so nice.

It was after nine o'clock when I arrived at the dining room. I had just spent an hour with Keith Garson and survived. Looking into his gorgeous blue eyes had been nearly impossible at first, but he had been so easygoing that I had been able to relax with him and learned a lot about cameras, too. Keith seemed like a really special guy. He had grown up totally gorgeous, and yet there was nothing stuck-up about him. He had been so patient with me, and he'd even offered to give me another lesson. But then, he'd seemed so relieved when the lesson was over. What was going on in his mind?

My parents were sitting in the dining room nursing their cups of coffee when I arrived. Greg was sitting at a nearby table with Jeremy Garson and another boy about their age.

"Good morning, Samantha, where have you been?" asked Mom.

"Keith Garson was giving me a photography lesson." I tried to keep my voice as matter-of-fact as I could.

"How did it go, pussycat?" asked Dad.

"It was fine. But I didn't realize how much I had to learn!"

"No one ever said it was simple," agreed Dad. "But then Keith is a more than willing teacher." I wasn't hungry, so I ordered coffee and orange juice from the waitress as Dad drained the last of his coffee. "Charlotte," he said to Mom, "I've got to dash down to check on the arrangements for the barbeque tonight, so I'll meet you on the tennis court in twenty minutes."

"I'll leave with you. I have to get our rackets and balls—and your hat." She laughed.

Meryl showed up just as my parents got up to go. "I see you've got a camera," Meryl said and cheerfully sat down beside me.

"It's Keith's," I confessed. "He gave me a photography lesson this morning."

"Was it really so awful? You sound like you're about to cry."

"Actually, Keith was just the opposite of awful. In fact, I hate to admit that I really do like him. And photography seems like it's going to be a lot of fun once I get the camera worked out."

"So what's the problem? I'd say you get an award for being such a fast worker with Keith."

"Meryl, please," I said, embarrassed.

"I'm just jealous," she confessed. "I wish I could figure out some way to get Tom to notice me so fast."

"You looked like you were doing pretty well last night."

"Yes, but what about today? I'm dying to find out what he's doing. Which of the millions of activities do you suppose he'll decide to attend?"

"Shh," I hissed. "Don't look now, but Tom and Jim just walked in, and they're sitting by the door."

The waitress brought my coffee and a juice. Meryl ordered orange juice. Then she turned to me. "So what do you think we should do today?"

I thought for a moment. "You know," I said finally, "I don't think I need those football lectures and aerobic classes. What I really want to do with my day is sit on the beach and get a fabulous tan."

"Sounds good to me," agreed Meryl. "But hold on a second," she said quietly. "I'm trying to eavesdrop on that conversation over there," she nodded toward the twins' table. "Then I'll know exactly what I want to do."

"Has anyone ever told you that you have a one-track mind? From this distance you'll never hear what they're saying."

Meryl's juice arrived, and she drank it quickly. "Let's say hello on the way out," she suggested quickly. As we walked over to the table, Tom waved to us heartily. "You missed a great time down at the beach this morning," he said. "Jim and I went down there to check out the running conditions, and who should we meet there but Keith and Candace." So that's why Keith was so eager to be rid of me.

"The beach is perfect for running," volunteered Jim.

"Do you run every morning?" Meryl asked.

"At home we do three and a half miles every day," said Tom. "And it looks like we'll be able to do the same here."

"Do you ever run, Samantha?" asked Jim with some hesitation in his voice.

"I was never very good at it. I'm really slow," I told him honestly.

"I've run a little at school," put in Meryl. "But never on a regular basis or anything. Is it hard?"

"Nothing to it," pronounced Tom.

"But you do have to build up slowly," offered Jim. "Maybe you'd like to run a little with us tomorrow morning." He looked from Meryl to me hopefully.

"Hey, thanks, that sounds like fun," Meryl said. "Well, we're off to the beach now."

"See you around," said Tom. "We're going to that football lecture Samantha told us about."

As we walked in the bright sun, Meryl said, "At least they'll know where we are. Maybe they'll come find us after the lecture."

"Maybe," I murmured, but I was too distracted to say much. I was thinking about how Keith had rushed away after our lesson. Now I knew he had gone to meet Candace.

I don't really care what Keith does, I told

myself. *And besides, I'm not going to let Candace Vale, or anyone else, get in the way of learning to be a good photographer. That's something I* know *I want to do.*

Chapter Six

Meryl and I easily found our way to the beach. We followed the tiled path through a garden of red and yellow flowers and into a path of palm trees. When the tiles ended and the path became sandy, I kicked off my shoes. We turned a corner, and there before us lay a long, white, powdery beach. The water was almost green by the shore, becoming a deeper blue farther out.

On one side of the path, white lounge chairs and tables were set up. Palm trees provided shade, and everyone looked very comfortable lying in the sun or splashing in the crystal waters. On the other side, the beach ran untouched for miles. There was not a sign of civilization to be seen.

Meryl and I dutifully coated ourselves with sunscreen. I admired Meryl's bathing suit. It was a purple one-piece that tied around her neck. We lay on the beach, quietly soaking up the peace. After a while we began chatting easily about our lives at home, our eyes closed against the sun. Soon Meryl sat up and got her watch out of her beach bag. "Good grief, we've been sitting here nearly an hour!" she exclaimed. "We've got to get out of the sun for a while, or we'll be as red as lobsters tonight. I hope it's not too late already."

"I feel fine," I told her.

"Good, but take my advice and quit while you're ahead."

We found two chairs under the shade of a palm tree, but I didn't feel like sitting around anymore. "I'm going for a walk down the beach," I said. "Want to join me?"

"No, thanks," she said, pulling a book out of her bag. "I think I'll hang out here. Put your shirt on. Your back doesn't need any more sun."

Taking Keith's camera, I considered the

panorama. There was a lot of activity at the water's edge, and I snapped off a few pictures, but somehow the long stretch of deserted beach beckoned to me.

I walked for a while along the shore, letting the cool water lap around my ankles. The beach curved, and the hotel and its inhabitants disappeared from sight. The view was stark and beautiful. But once I had taken a few pictures, there didn't seem to be any more to do. *Snapshots*, I complained to myself.

I was considering turning back when I saw what looked like a boat up in the bushes. On the off chance that it would be a good subject for a photo, I headed across the sand to investigate.

In the low, green shrubbery that bordered the beach, there was a sandy clearing with a large-leafed shade tree standing to one side. Underneath the tree were five or six bulky wooden boats, each painted in a different color combination. They looked as if they'd weathered a few storms. I felt sure that the shapes of the boats and their textures would make an interesting photograph.

Circling my subject slowly, my eye to the camera, I concentrated on choosing an angle and a distance that would capture the boats best. I wasn't sure exactly what to do. *Look, focus, snap, look, focus,* I told myself calmly. Then when I was satisfied that I had tried all the interesting angles, I put the lens cover back on the camera, closed up the case, and headed back to find Meryl.

"Hey," I called when I spotted her purple suit, "I think I got some good pictures of a few old boats that are beached around the bend."

"Oh, no, don't tell me you're going to turn into one of those serious photography types. Just when we were starting to have a good time!"

"Well, it was fun and serious at the same time," I explained.

"I'd love to see your photos," she said, "even though I'm not about to rush out with a camera myself. Hey, will you look who's coming over here," she said enthusiastically. I turned, half hoping it would be Keith, to find the twins jogging toward us.

"Hello, you two," called Tom.

"How was the football lecture?" Meryl asked.

Jim laughed. "We really enjoyed it, but frankly we'd rather be playing the sport than talking about it."

"We were thinking of doing a little wind

surfing this afternoon, and we thought you might want to come," Tom said, smiling broadly.

"I don't even know what wind surfing is," I admitted.

"Well, the equipment's kind of like a surfboard with a sail," he told me.

"Sounds hard," I said.

"Don't worry, I'll teach you to sail like a pro," offered Jim.

"I'd like to give it a try," Meryl said. "Let's skip lunch and go now."

"Sure," I agreed. "This camera has been in the sun too much today, but I guess I could leave it in the sailing house."

Meryl and I gathered up our things, and then the four of us headed down the beach to the sailing house. As we walked along the shore, we met Candace coming in the opposite direction. She was looking gorgeous in a revealing white maillot bathing suit, and she had a red flower tucked behind her ear.

"Hey, where's Keith?" Tom asked, as if she were the expert.

"He went over to Grande Case early this morning," she announced in a knowing voice that I didn't like one bit.

"We're going wind surfing. Want to come?" Jim asked.

"Oh, I've always wanted to learn that sport," she said, tossing her blond hair behind her. "I'd love to come."

Somehow, Jim ended up teaching Candace a whole lot more than he did me. I gave the strange surfboard a few halfhearted attempts, then spent the rest of the afternoon under a shady palm tree. Keith didn't appear all day. It wasn't until dinner that I saw him in the dining room with his family. And I didn't even get to talk to him then. He left quickly after dessert without a word to me.

Paradise Bay was having a Ping-Pong tournament, and Meryl, the twins, and I had decided earlier to sign up. We went for a little practice after the meal and played a good game of doubles. I'm a real whiz at Ping-Pong, and I racked up more points than anyone else.

Shortly after our first game, Keith arrived with Candace. They came over and said hi, then found a free table and began playing. They were both really good, and they laughed a lot as the evening progressed. Needless to say, I didn't enjoy watching them together. I mean, I had a good time with Meryl and the twins, but my eyes and thoughts kept wandering to the table across the room.

By the time I went back to the room it was eleven-thirty, and Greg was sound asleep. Just to be on the safe side, I locked myself in the bathroom before I began my nightly diary entry. Frustrated by my feelings for Keith and exhausted by the day's events, I wrote in big, sloppy handwriting. Aside from a little friendly chitchat, Keith hadn't bothered to communicate with me all evening.

It was funny how my ideas about Keith had changed in one day. First I'd dreaded meeting him because he had been such a creep. Then I became terrified to talk to him because he turned out to be so attractive. And now I was really upset because he seemed to be avoiding me. He had been so friendly and easygoing during our lesson, and then he had ignored me for the rest of the day. If only I had been able to apologize back at Montauk. Well, I had a second photography lesson the next morning. I'd see what would happen then.

I awoke early the next morning and got dressed quietly. I put turquoise shorts and a white cotton net shirt over my bathing suit. If only I had a flower for my hair. *What hair*? I said to myself bitterly. Mine was only half an inch long. Besides, what was the use? I'd never look like Candace.

As I walked to the pool, I realized how nervous I was. Keith, on the other hand, looked just as relaxed as he had the day before. "Here are the contact sheets of the shots I took at the airport," he said, pulling a piece of paper out of a large white envelope. Handing me a flashlight with a magnifying glass attached, he showed me how to look at the thirty-six tiny black-and-white pictures. "These were made for me by Paul Bostwick, a free-lance photographer who lives here on the island."

I studied the mob scene, which he had photographed from so high up. "Wow!" I exclaimed. "These really capture the hustle and bustle of the airport. I almost feel as if I'm there again."

I looked up and saw Keith smiling. "Thanks," he said, "I was hoping you would say something like that."

"But the pictures are so tiny," I commented. "Wouldn't they be easier to see if they were larger?"

"Right you are." He laughed easily. "The next step is to study the sheets and pick out two or three of the best pictures. Some are obviously much better than others, and those are the ones I'll enlarge when I get back home to my darkroom. How did your shooting go yesterday?"

"Great—I think." I told him about the boats I had found on the beach.

"Sounds promising. If you give me your film, I'll ask Paul to develop it."

"That would be great, except I have eight exposures left," I told him, checking the number indicator on the camera.

"No problem. Just shoot them off now."

"Well, uh, I guess I could take more pictures of the pool."

"Have you photographed any people yet?"

"Just a few shots on the beach. It seemed kind of hard," I confessed. "They move!"

"Yes," he agreed, smiling. "But portraiture is a whole other area that you should get to know. I'll tell you what. Since no one else is around to pose, you can use me. I'll sit very still, I promise."

"Thanks," I muttered. It had been hard enough getting myself to keep cool while we talked. Now he wanted me to focus my camera on him.

We chose a comfortable chair for him to sit in, and I scrutinized him carefully through the camera. He had a relaxed expression on his face, but it seemed to mask some deeper emotion. It took me more than a few seconds to get over my nervousness at looking at Keith Garson in the viewfinder, but eventually I was able to concentrate on my shots. I was glad that I was safely hidden behind the camera.

"I think I'm done," I told him finally.

"Fine. Let me show you how to rewind the film and unload it. Then you can put in another roll while I'm still here to help."

I appreciated his thoughtfulness, but I didn't much like the idea that this might be the only time all day that he would talk to me. For a moment I considered pretending to be confused about what I was doing. It was fun huddling over the camera with Keith. But honesty won out, and I loaded the camera with impressive ease.

"What are you going to shoot today?" Keith asked.

"Maybe I'll walk farther down the beach and see what else there is."

"Good idea," he approved. "But don't be afraid to try moving subjects. You'll get used to focusing quickly once you practice. Just be sure to shoot off a lot of shots when you find something you like. It's the only way to learn."

"So you've been telling me," I said.

"We'll see how you're doing when we get the contacts back. I'll let you know at the Ping-Pong tournament tonight if your sheets are ready. Otherwise, let's meet here at the same time tomorrow." He got up to leave, and there was little I could do to make the lesson last longer.

"Great, thanks," I told him. "And good luck tonight. You and Candace looked excellent last night, so I'm assuming you'll be in the tournament, too."

"Yes," he confirmed. "And you looked like a pretty good player yourself." So he had watched me a little bit. Well, I'd have to be content with that. With a smile and a wave, Keith turned his back on me and headed for the beach.

Meryl and I played Ping-Pong that morning with Tom and Jim. At first we played doubles, and then we took turns playing singles. Meryl was just an average player, and she was practicing more to be near Tom than anything else. Jim turned out to be a great player, and we had a few good, fast games. But I was getting uneasy about the way Jim looked at me. I wondered if he thought our friendship was more special than I did.

Eventually the four of us made our way to the beach to swim, lie around, and tell stupid knock-knock jokes. It was a perfect sunny afternoon, full of giggling and laughter. The only thing that would have made it nicer was if Keith had been there.

By midafternoon I was ready to do some camera work. "I'm going for a walk down the beach," I told my friends as I removed Keith's camera from my tote bag. "Anyone want to come?" I asked the question out of politeness. I'd intended to go by myself, but Jim got up, too.

"I'll come, Samantha."

"Fine, but I'm going with the idea of finding something to photograph. I won't be much fun to talk to."

"No problem, but there's not much down there."

"Yesterday I found a beautiful pile of old boats quite by accident," I explained as we started to walk. "I'm hoping to stumble on something else like that."

"As far as I've seen, there's nothing down at the far end but a lot of rocks and an old swamp," said Jim.

We walked along the powdery beach, talking quietly about our schools and hometowns. All the while my eyes were searching for an interesting subject. "I can't believe how far we've come," I told Jim. "Where's that swamp you were talking about?"

"Right beyond that bend. It's not much, really." We walked silently up the hot sand, the sun beating down on us. I was beginning to think that I wasn't going to find anything to shoot.

But when we reached Jim's "swamp," really a mossy clearing hidden in the tall grasses, I quickly changed my mind. To one side was a small pond, and there was an enormous blue-gray bird standing in the water on long, stiltlike legs. I tapped Jim on the arm, and he nodded his head silently. I began to focus my camera, hoping like crazy that the bird wouldn't be frightened off by the clicking of the shutter. Except for the lapping of the Caribbean and the call of birds, there were no other sounds.

Jim stood still as I took my shots. The camera noise seemed as loud as fireworks to me, but the bird didn't seem to mind. As I worked, several small, white birds landed in the pond, too, and began to fish. I focused quickly, knowing my subjects wouldn't cooperate long. Finally I was done; I tapped Jim on the arm again, and we tiptoed back to the beach. The birds, miraculously, remained undisturbed.

"Wow, wasn't that something. Thanks a lot, Jim," I burst out as soon as we were well away.

"I'm glad you liked it. But if you ask me, it looked like your basic run-of-the-mill swamp."

"But the water was so glassy and still, and that big bird was so majestic."

Jim just shrugged.

As we walked back toward the hotel, I tried to figure out why I wasn't attracted to Jim the way I was to Keith. He was tall and well-built with shiny, brown, curly hair and a cute face. He was certainly friendly. But there was more to it than that. Keith had a positive attitude that seemed really unique. I had never met anyone like him before. Jim was just another nice guy.

"How was your trip?" asked Meryl when we arrived back at the lounge chairs. "You two looked so romantic walking off into the distance."

"I took Samantha to a cozy little swamp I know," said Jim jokingly.

"It was terrific, I got some great shots!" I said enthusiastically.

"Oh, Samantha, you're becoming so serious, like a real photographer," she said teasingly.

I could only smile. "It's a great feeling," I told her.

Chapter Seven

I had no trouble making it into the final round of the Paradise Bay Ping-Pong tournament that night, but as I stood across the net from Candace, the other finalist, I knew I was in for trouble. Dressed in her designer outfit, she had a look that said, "I am determined to win."

Let me say that I played an excellent game, but Candace finally demolished me at 27 to 29. It was a real letdown, as you can imagine, but it wasn't until she nodded her head at the spectators, who were clapping politely, and stalked away without so much as a handshake that I felt really angry.

Meryl and Jim rushed up to congratulate me on the hard game I had just played. After all, as Meryl reminded me, in the big picture Ping-Pong would always be just Ping-Pong. I appreciated Meryl's little philosophical tidbit. But later, as I stood in the crowd waiting to congratulate Jim on beating Keith for the title of men's division champ, I couldn't help focusing on what seemed to me to be the truly big picture: Candace and Keith walking off together, Candace with that ever-familiar smirk on her face.

The next morning at my photography lesson, Keith said, "Well, we both got one-upped last night, didn't we?" He grinned. "But it was fun, anyway, didn't you think?"

I nodded my head. To anyone else I could have complained about Candace's poor sportsmanship, but to Keith it might have sounded like sour grapes.

"So do you want to see your contacts? I think you're going to be very happy with them," he said. He handed me a sheet of tiny black-and-white pictures like the one he'd shown me the day before.

My first reaction was shock. After all, what I had seen through the viewfinder of the camera was in vivid tropical color. What I held in my hand was a lifeless gray. At least, it seemed that way at first. "Uh," I said, "I totally forgot I was taking black-and-white pictures." If I had wanted to impress him with my sophisticated nonchalance, I had just failed miserably.

"Black and white does take some getting used to," he acknowledged, "but I think you'll be surprised if you take a close look at what's there."

As I studied the little pictures with the magnifying glass, I began to see the character of the boats with their awkward shapes and bumpy textures.

"You've got some very nice-looking shots, especially for a first roll. You should be very proud of yourself."

"Thanks," I told him, suddenly unable to tear my eyes away from the sheet. The scene looked almost more dramatic in black and white.

"Do you have any favorites?" he asked.

"I definitely like this one of the three boats best," I answered easily. "But wait. Am I imagining it, or are they slightly out of focus?"

"Let me have a look." Keith was silent for a

few seconds as he studied the pictures in question. "I think you're right," he said finally. "They are just a bit soft. Too bad."

"I can't believe it!" My disappointment was obvious.

"But it was your first time with a camera, and you're just learning how to focus," he reminded me. "Besides you've got something much more important happening here. Your composition is really good, and that counts for a lot more."

"Maybe the boats will still be there this afternoon," I thought out loud. "I could try it again."

"Way to go," he said encouragingly.

"Gee," I went on, "I took some pictures down the beach yesterday of some fabulous birds. I hope I got those right because I doubt I can get them to pose for me again."

"We'll have to wait and see."

"Do you think Paul Bostwick will develop more film?" I asked skeptically.

"I don't see why not."

"Is he a special friend of yours?"

"I met him when we checked into Paradise Bay. He was hanging his show in the main building and we got to talking about photography. Since then, we've been out shooting together twice. He's a great guy. He earns his living by taking pictures at a lot of the big hotels, and he has his own darkroom."

"Wow. I've never actually seen a darkroom," I told him. Keith looked surprised. "I've never had any interest in photography before, and Dad's into the selling end of cameras. I mean, he does photography, but he doesn't develop his own film."

"Darkrooms are like magic. They're absolutely fascinating." Keith positively bubbled with enthusiasm. "I'll tell you what. I'll ask Paul if I can bring you over for a darkroom tour."

"That would be great!"

We talked a bit more about photographic composition and special effects. But when the lesson was over, Keith politely excused himself and took off alone, leaving me both excited by what we had talked about and confused by his cool goodbye. With a shrug, I headed for the dining room, hoping to find Meryl.

"You know," I complained to her as we sat having our breakfast, "photography is the beginning and the end of what Keith has to say to me. As soon as we're done, he takes off and won't speak to me until the next lesson."

"What does he do all day?" she asked.

"Photography stuff, I think, but I'm not exactly sure. For all I know, he's hanging out with Candace."

"Too bad for him if he's got such bad taste," she responded frankly. "Besides, Sam, I can't figure out why you're so hung up on the guy. I admit he's really cute and all, but he seems to have a one-track mind. Remember what we decided about those photography types. They're too serious."

"But Keith is such a nice kind of serious," I explained, and I couldn't help thinking of his gentle enthusiasm and warm voice.

"Oh, pooh," she scoffed. "What you need is to have fun with me and Tom and Jim. Jim is really good-looking, and he likes you, in case you hadn't noticed.

"I sort of had," I admitted. "And don't get me wrong, I like Jim a lot—"

"But he's not Keith," she finished for me.

"No," I confirmed, "he's not Keith."

"But you will come play Frisbee on the big lawn with the twins and me this morning, won't you?"

"Thanks, Meryl, but as soon as I'm done I'm rushing down to the beach to see if those boats are still there."

"What'll I tell Jim?" she wanted to know.

"The truth. There was something else I had planned to do, take pictures." Meryl shook her head. "Come on. No guilt trips," I said as we stood up to head off in our own directions.

I practically ran down the beach to the clearing where the boats had been. They were still there, untouched, and I was relieved and excited. At first I tried to stand exactly where I had stood the time before, but then I realized it would be impossible to get the same shots. Instead, I decided to start from the beginning, taking whatever seemed interesting, focusing slowly and carefully.

It was really fun to look through the viewfinder and discover new angles. This time I looked even harder at the shapes and textures of the boat, the trees and the sand. I knew that I couldn't rely on the glamour of color to make my pictures work.

Before long, the frame indicator told me I had finished up the thirty-six shots on the roll. I had worked for more than a half an hour, and I felt exhilarated and exhausted at the same time.

I walked up the beach toward the hotel to see if Meryl and the twins were still on the big lawn. They were a lot of fun, and I should have been looking forward to seeing them, yet I didn't really feel like it. They seemed to talk about the same things over and over. What I really wanted to do was sit down with Keith and have a real conversation. I knew I would be quite satisfied to talk to him about photography all afternoon.

As it turned out, Meryl and the twins weren't still playing Frisbee, but they'd left me a note, saying they had decided to go wind surfing again. They were still in the water when I got to the sailing house, so I stood at the water's edge and watched them struggle with the absence of wind. "Coming in?" called Jim as he sat on his stationary board. "The water's great!"

The sun was really hot, I realized, without a hint of the cooling breeze of the previous day. I couldn't wait to get in the water. After wrapping Keith's camera carefully in my towel and tucking the bundle into my beach bag, I went racing in.

At first the water felt cool and tingly, but as I swam toward the sunbathing float that was anchored several yards offshore, it began to feel deliciously warm. I climbed onto the float, then spread out in the heat of the sun. The gentle bobbing motion of the float felt calming, lulling me into a pleasant half sleep.

"Hello," said a familiar voice, interrupting my catnap. Jim pulled himself up the steps onto the float. "How was your walk?"

"Just fine," I told him. "Those old boats were still there, so I got to take more pictures of them."

"Once wasn't enough?" he said, pushing his hand through his dripping wet hair.

"I messed up the first time around," I explained. "And I wanted to try again."

"Then I'm glad you found what you wanted. To tell you the truth, Samantha, I really am impressed by all this photography stuff. Tom and I took it for a semester in school, and I wasn't much good at it."

"How come?" I asked. "It's not physically difficult."

"That's for sure," he said and laughed. "No, it's something completely different. My pictures were nothing special, just pictures, if you know what I mean. I did my assignments and passed OK, but I never came up with anything great. I was just glad when the course was over."

"That's too bad."

"I guess," he answered. "But at least now I know a bit about photography. Anyway, I'm sorry if I sometimes make fun of what you're doing. I really do understand that some people see things that I don't."

"Gee, that's OK, Jim." I was touched by his words.

"So, listen," he went on quickly, as if he might lose his nerve, "Friday is the snorkel trip out to Sandy Island. Want to go?"

"Sure, except I've never been snorkeling before in my life."

"But I can see you're a good swimmer, and there'll be lessons in the pool before we go. Tom and Meryl are coming. It's going to be really great."

Before I knew it, I had agreed. But had I made a mistake? I wasn't afraid of snorkeling, but I *was* afraid of what was happening to my friendship with Jim. I didn't want him to think of this as a real date or anything.

But as it turned out, I was glad to have Jim's invitation. After more swimming and a quick Frisbee game, Meryl, Tom, Jim, and I were lying on our lounge chairs on the beach, talking and kidding around, when Keith and Candace suddenly appeared. Keith was his usual gorgeous self in a black racing suit, and Candace looked impressively coordinated in her matching bathing suit, wraparound skirt, and hat. We were all starting to have great tans, but somehow, Candace looked darker than the rest of us.

"Look what the tide washed in," said Tom, joking.

"The shopping is just great in Marigot," Candace announced.

"Really," responded Meryl. "What did you get?"

"Well, the perfume is really cheap here because it's duty free. So I just had to stock up on Shalimar. And I ended up buying so much that Keith had to give me a ride home in that cute little rented car of his. Wasn't it lucky that he passed by at just the right time?"

Oh, brother, is this the kind of girl Keith really likes? I wondered. *Maybe I've misjudged him after all!* I tried to console myself with what Meryl had called his incredible bad taste. But it was no use. I was still jealous.

"What else is there in Marigot?" pursued Meryl.

"A darling shop with the most wonderful shell jewelry made by an island artist. And it's so cheap, you'll never believe it."

It would have killed me to admit that I was interested in anything Candace had to say, so I kept my mouth shut and let my mind wander while Meryl pumped her for more shopping tips. I was trying to figure out what made Candace tick when someone said my name softly. Looking up, I found Keith sitting on the sand next to me.

"All set," he said quietly, pride in his voice. "Paul says we can come around to his place tomorrow morning."

"Wow. That's great."

"Be sure to finish up one roll of film, or more if you can, and bring it along."

"No problem. I went back and reshot a whole roll of those boats. I hope I got them this time," I added.

"We'll get a look tomorrow."

"I can hardly wait. Hey, how many rolls have you shot?"

"Probably ten or twelve, but I'll just pick out a couple for Paul's tank and do the rest when I get home."

"Amazing," I said, impressed by how hard Keith was working. "What have you been shooting? You've never told me about what you do. It's not all airport stuff is it?"

"No," he said. "I didn't tell you what I was doing because I didn't want to influence what you chose. There's so much here, I wanted you to look for yourself."

"Thanks," I said, smiling, "but now I'm really curious!"

"Tomorrow when we develop the rolls, you'll get a look."

"Hey, campers," Tom called out, "our next activity is swimming. Everyone down to the water, and the last one in is a rotten egg."

That ended my conversation with Keith. We all stood up and ran like crazy across the sand. All of us except Candace, that is. She was too busy folding up her coordinated skirt. For a few minutes I could actually forget she was there and have a lot of fun laughing and splashing in the clear blue Caribbean with Keith.

Chapter Eight

Meryl seemed to have succeeded in her quest to spend time with Tom. They danced together that night at Splashes, oblivious to the rest of the world, leaving Jim, Keith, Candace, and me to switch off with one another. It was fun, and I had a great time. Except whenever Keith and Candace danced together, I wanted to scream. It wasn't that he didn't dance with me, because he did. I was just supersensitive to every moment he spent with her. I tried as hard as I could not to let my feelings show, but I was glad when the evening was finally over and I could complain to my diary.

The next morning Keith and I met at seven-thirty for our trip to Paul Bostwick's dark-room. "It's at least a half hour to Paul's, and he has to leave by eleven for a shooting," he said as we headed out to the parking lot.

Candace had been partially accurate in her description of Keith's car. It was little and cute, but she had forgotten to mention that it had no roof.

"What do you do when it rains?" I asked, buckling my seat belt.

"Get wet," he said, joking. "Actually, there's a top folded up in the back. "Are you worried about your hair?"

"Are you kidding? With *this* haircut?" I told him about my accident with the red paint at school, and he laughed. I even found myself laughing.

"Your hair *is* short," he acknowledged. "But it's not that hard to get used to." I couldn't tell by his tone or his funny smile exactly what he meant, and I didn't have the nerve to ask.

"Thanks," I said quietly. Maybe he was just being polite. Even so, that was more than I'd been at Montauk. If I had been brave enough to apologize for that past incident, it would have been the perfect moment. But I was such a coward, I kept my mouth shut.

Keith drove through the busy little town of Marigot and into the country—up and down hills that were so big they might have been called mountains. We rode past tiny houses, many no better than shacks, each painted in a different, but beautiful, combination of pink, green, and blue. We cruised next to fields bordered with stone walls and inhabited by cows and goats, as well as down lanes blooming with overgrown, brilliantly colored flowers.

It was the first time I had left the manicured luxury of the hotel since we'd arrived, and the trip was a real eye-opener. "Life at the hotel is certainly different from life out here in the real world," I observed. Up ahead was a flock of goats walking along the edge of the road. "Seeing all this makes Paradise Bay seem so excessive. It just doesn't feel right that we should be living in such luxury, with too much of everything, while these people have so very little. It's awful to realize that a whole family lives in just one tiny house."

"I agree," he told me. "The richness of Paradise Bay bothers me, too. But we're here, so we'll just have to enjoy it as much as we can. My own choice would have been someplace a little more in keeping with the way the island people live."

"Yes, but somehow I can't see Globex people getting into that," I answered, and we both laughed.

"Think on the positive side," he said. "There are a lot of jobs at the hotel for island people, and that's good. Meantime don't start feeling guilty, or you'll never have a good time."

Keith had driven the car up a long, rocky path that had me clutching my seat. I was glad our seat belts were holding us safely in the car, and I felt relieved when we finally reached a neat, white, two-story house set on a long, sloping lawn. Paul Bostwick came down the steep front steps to greet us. I had to smile as I finally met the photographer about whom I had once had such dreamy fantasies. A slight, attractive man in his midthirties, he had a deep, rich tan on the top of his balding head.

"I hear you've come for your first lesson in darkroom technique," he said, smiling. The twinkle in his eyes and the warmth in his voice made me feel welcome right away.

"Yes, if you don't mind," I answered, embarrassed to be such a beginner.

"My pleasure," he told me. "Actually Keith

here is going to do the teaching. I'm just the landlord. Now, since time is so short, I think we should get started right away, so follow me."

He directed us to a door that led into the lower floor of his house. Then we entered a small room furnished simply, a few canvas chairs and with colorful woven mats on the floor. The walls were hung with clusters of black-and-white photographs. I was anxious to look at them closely, but Paul began to explain about the darkroom, which took all my concentration. He showed me a large, stainless-steel cylinder that was a developing tank for film. Opening one end, he pulled out a circular wire form.

"The film has to be loaded on this in the absolute dark," he explained. "Then, once it's developed and dried, you can begin to make prints in the darkroom with a special safe light. I'll show you quickly how to load the tank out here with a dummy roll, and I'll let Keith do the actual loading inside."

Taking a roll of film from a nearby table, he deftly threaded it onto the wire reel. "If the film touches itself," he explained, "there will be blank spots on the negatives." Paul smiled as he wound up the last of the film. "Eh, voilà," he announced.

"Don't let Paul fool you," Keith told me. "That particular style of reel takes a lot of practice. I remember blowing quite a few rolls before I got it worked out."

"OK, Keith, you're all set. Load up the tank with your stuff, and then Samantha can join you."

I handed Keith my roll of film, and he disappeared behind the curtain.

"Keith is something," Paul told me. "We've been spending some time together shooting and printing. I'm really going to miss him when his vacation is over, not that he's had much of a rest."

"You'd be surprised," yelled Keith from behind the curtain. "And just in case you were planning to say anything else about me, I can hear every word you're saying."

Paul and I laughed, and I turned to look at the black-and-white photographs hanging behind us. They were portraits of dark-skinned Saint Martin people standing in front of their homes. Some of the buildings looked very roomy and comfortable, while others were shacks similar to those I had just seen. I studied the photographs, thinking at first about how poor so many of the islanders were. But the longer I looked, the more I began to see strong, handsome, proud people who made the best of what they had. It was a deeply moving experience.

"Paul, your photographs are so beautiful I can hardly take my eyes off them," I said breathlessly.

"Thank you, Samantha. I'm delighted that you like them."

"All set," called Keith from behind the curtain.

"In you go," directed Paul. "I'll be back to see your prints."

I don't know what I expected a darkroom to look like, but I was definitely surprised to find myself in a tiny room dimly lit with a reddish light. Along one wall was a counter that held a sink, several black, plastic trays, and a funny-looking machine that Keith said was the enlarger. On the wall above was a big square clock with luminous numbers. There were also shelves filled with cans of chemicals and other odd-looking containers.

Keith explained what he was doing as he poured a clear liquid into the silver container of film. Watching the clock, he then shook the chemicals gently at evenly spaced intervals.

After changing the liquids several times, he proclaimed the film developed. Again, I wasn't quite sure what I expected. Opening the canisters, he took out strips of dark film and hung them on a clothesline to dry.

"This is your film," he told me, pointing to a strip. "If you're careful to touch only the edges, you can take a look at what you've got." He was studying my film himself. "The emulsion looks good," he announced.

"What does that mean?"

"Good exposures, with the right amount of light. It shouldn't be hard to get good prints."

"How do we do that?"

"Ah, now that's where the fun comes in. I just want to take a few minutes to look at my own negatives, and we'll get started."

I was disappointed to learn that the film I had just watched develop would have to dry for a half hour or so before we could print it. Hanging like spaghetti on a clothesline, it may have meant something to Keith, but to me it was still a mystery.

While we were waiting, Keith pulled out of his camera bag a skinny envelope that contained other strips of developed film. Choosing one, he inserted it into the enlarger. He turned on the light in the machine and brought the picture into focus on a white metal board. "Now this is the most magical of all," he promised. He switched off the enlarger light and fitted the paper onto the metal easel. When he turned the enlarger back on, the clock on the wall began to run.

We stood together and listened to the clock tick off the seconds. Then a buzzer sounded, and the enlarger light shut off automatically. Keith removed the blank paper and slipped it into one of the trays of clear liquid. "Keep your eyes on the paper," he told me as he switched on the clock.

Magic was the word Keith had used, and magic it seemed. Watching the picture come out slowly on the paper as it soaked in the developing bath, it was hard to believe that a print could just appear like that on a blank piece of paper.

"Isn't that something. I still get the same thrill when I watch images come up," said Keith, grinning at me. With plastic tongs, he moved the picture into first one tray and then another.

"Tell me what happened. What are in all these trays?"

Keith patiently described the developing liquid, the bath to stop the developing, and the chemical to fix the image. "These are just the barest basics," he warned. Then he handed me the print. "Take a look at this even though it really needs a lot of work." It was one of his airport shots.

"It doesn't seem like it needs work to me," I said.

"This spot near the luggage area didn't come up as much as it should have, so next time I'll have to burn it in. This crowd of people over here came up too quickly and got too dense. I should be able to take care of that, too."

I watched with fascination as Keith worked systematically to make a new and better print. It was an incredible process. I could have watched him all day. But he kept close tabs on the time outside in the real world so we wouldn't overstay our visit.

We talked photography nonstop during the car ride back to the hotel. In our first lessons together, I'd felt like Keith was overwhelming me with technical information. This time, I kept bombarding him with questions.

We got back to the hotel in time for lunch, and I felt great walking into the dining room with Keith and sitting down at the table with Meryl, the twins, and Candace. I think I was actually grinning from ear to ear, though Keith seemed like his usual, calm self.

"If it isn't Clark Kent and Lois Lane," greeted Tom.

"Welcome back to Metropolis," added Candace with none of Tom's friendliness. "How about a ride down to Marigot later, Keith?" she purred. I waited for his response, wishing he would tell her off.

"Actually, I am going that way about twoish," he said. "But I promised a friend I'd help him with a photography job out in Oyster Pond, so you'll have to take the hotel minibus back. It leaves every hour from the post office."

I could detect no special warmth in his voice. "There's more room in the car. Does anyone else want a lift?" Keith asked.

Meryl and Tom, deciding this was the perfect opportunity to check out the shops Candace had told them about, quickly took him up on his offer.

"Samantha, do you want a ride?" Keith asked.

"Maybe I'll bring my camera to town and do some shooting," I answered.

"Good idea," he approved. "Jim, a ride, too?"

Jim, who had remained silent so far, finally decided to join the group. Had he been influenced, I wondered, by my decision? But I couldn't let it worry me for long. I was getting too excited about taking pictures.

Chapter Nine

We all piled into Keith's car for our ride into Marigot. Candace managed to claim the front seat, and the rest of us squeezed into the back. Watching her flip her hair confidently over her shoulder, I reached up to feel my own hair, so short and now wavy from the Caribbean air. It was funny. Since we had come to Saint Martin, I was starting to feel comfortable, even happy with the way I looked. My great suntan helped, of course, but I was even beginning to like my short hair. It was definitely more grown up and stylish than my long hair had been. Mom had been right. It was more flattering to my face.

Meryl, Candace, and Tom were excitedly discussing the great bargains they were expecting to find while I kept scanning the countryside for pictures I'd like to take. I wished I could talk with Keith as we passed by a cluster of tiny, new, concrete houses being built by a marshy pond. I thought it would make an interesting photograph, with a real contrast of textures. Keith would certainly have an opinion. But from where I sat, wedged in the backseat of a tiny car in the middle of an already-too-loud conversation, there was no way I could start one of my own.

Keith dropped us at the edge of town and drove off into the hills before I could say any more than thank you. Candace led Meryl and Tom away to the jewelry store, leaving Jim standing by my side.

"I really do intend to do some shooting," I reminded him, patting the camera that hung around my neck. "Are you sure you wouldn't rather go shopping with the other guys?"

"No, I'd rather keep you company. If you don't mind?"

"But aren't you sorry you didn't bring a

camera, too? Everything looks so interesting."

"I'm happy to keep all the pictures of this place tucked up here." He tapped his temple with his finger. "Just lead on, I'll follow."

I couldn't have wished for a more pleasant companion. He was perfectly happy as I led him past fancy boutiques and restaurants to the bustling, inelegant waterfront. Actually, it wasn't my usual style to walk past all those shop windows without so much as a second look. But by now the possibility of getting some interesting shots was much more attractive to me than looking at clothes or souvenirs.

We stood on the dock, watching two men unload heavy crates. Jim was quiet as I looked through the viewfinder of the camera and chose the best angles. I shot nearly half a roll of film, using every ounce of concentration I had to focus quickly but sharply. I was worried that the men might object to my photographing them, but they seemed too busy to mind. When I was finished, Jim and I continued up the dock together, watching Saint Martin life around us.

"You're really weird," Jim said finally. "Of all

the things to take pictures of, you pick decrepit old boats and men lifting crates."

"What would you take?" I asked, too satisfied with my work to be put off by his criticism.

"Well," he started, "you know I'm not much into photography, but I would have found something pretty, like that bridge over there, with the town behind it. Now that's a Saint Martin scene to remember."

It was a real picture postcard view, and certainly worthy of a snapshot. "Let's walk a little closer, and I'll take a picture of you in front of it," I suggested.

"Great," he agreed.

By the time the afternoon was over, I had taken two and a half rolls of film while Jim cheerfully stood by. As we walked toward the post office to meet the others and catch the bus, he suddenly got very serious.

"I guess this would have been more fun for you if Keith had been with you," he said.

"Well, I probably would have learned a lot about photography, but I'm sure I'll never get the chance to take a walk like this with Keith."

"Why not?"

"I don't know, he keeps busy doing other things."

"That's dumb," he told me. "It's obvious that you two would have a good time taking pictures of all the boring stuff around here."

"It's not boring!"

"See, the only other person around here who would agree with you is Keith. Now he's an OK guy. But I've got to say he takes this photography stuff a little too far. And so do you, Samantha. Going snorkeling tomorrow is going to be good for you. It'll broaden your horizons, take your mind off photography for a while."

I had to smile at Jim's concern. The thing was, I didn't want anything to take my mind off photography or Keith. I just wanted to snap more and more pictures, and I wanted to see more and more of Keith.

We met up with Meryl, Tom, and Candace as we had arranged, and caught the Paradise Bay minibus back to the hotel. Meryl and Tom wore matching white-shell chokers around their necks and big grins across their faces. They really looked like a couple. Candace was carrying a shopping bag filled with perfumed soap, which she told me she had regretted not buying the day before.

It wasn't until dinner that I realized I hadn't seen my family all day. It was a great feeling to be so independent—a new feeling. At Paradise Bay, for the first time in my life, I was free to do exactly what I wanted without checking in with my parents. If they hadn't insisted that the family sit together for dinner, we might never have seen one another at all except to say hello as we passed in a hall or on the beach. They had been keeping closer tabs on Greg, much to his annoyance, because he was a lot younger. I was thrilled that they thought I was mature enough to take care of myself.

When I told my family about my visit with Keith to Paul Bostwick's darkroom, they were very impressed. "I've got to hand it to that boy," Dad commented. "He really knows his photographic techniques. His work must be good if Paul Bostwick is so impressed with him. Paul is a fine, fine photographer, and the Museum of Modern Art has just bought some of his prints for their permanent collection."

"The pictures hanging in his studio are spectacular," I told them. "And he's such a nice guy."

"Have you taken advantage of any of the hotel activities?" Dad asked.

"I've been on the beach a lot. The ocean is spectacular."

"Can we come back when I'm twelve so I can go wind surfing?" Greg wanted to know.

"We'll see," said Dad.

"Anyway, Dad," I continued, "I'm going on that snorkel trip to Sandy Island tomorrow."

"Sandy Island," wailed Greg. "It's supposed to be really neat. Since Sam's going, can I go, too? Please?"

"Sorry, Greg, I'm afraid that's going to have to wait until you're a little older, too," said Dad. "That's another activity for kids over twelve."

"Not if Samantha says I can come with her. What do you say, Sam? You're a good swimmer. You could watch out for me."

"I'm going to be learning to snorkel myself," I told him. "Maybe next time." Baby-sitting for Greg was the last thing in the world I wanted to do.

"But who knows when that'll be?"

"Greg," suggested Mom, "I've heard people talking about a nice reef out in front of the hotel. Why don't you snorkel there tomorrow where the lifeguard can watch you? Sam can't possibly look after you while she's a beginner herself."

"Thanks a lot, Sam," complained Greg.

"Remind me to do something nice for you sometime."

After dinner I played Ping-Pong with Meryl, Tom, Keith, Jim, and Candace. We set up our own little minitournament of singles and mixed doubles. I had a lot of fun except that Keith hardly said anything to me besides stuff like "Nice serve" or "Good volley." I kept hoping he'd say something just a little more personal, something to show he thought I was special. The less he said, the more anxious I felt. And by the end of the evening, I really thought I was going to go crazy.

For a while Greg, Jeremy Garson, and two other kids took the table next to ours, and I could feel Greg watching us. We were playing a fast game, and I thought he must be pretty impressed. Looking back on it, though, I think he had something else in mind.

As I wrote in my diary that night, I decided it had been both a good day and a not-so-good day for me. Sitting alone in the tiled bathroom with my diary *did* help me sort out my thoughts. First of all, I was vacationing in one of the most beautiful places in the world and being given more independence than I had ever had before. Then why did I feel rotten half the time? The biggest problem was Keith. All I really wanted to do was spend more time with him. My feelings for him were more than just a passing crush, I was sure. I wanted to be near him and to talk to him about everything and anything in the world. He, on the other hand, just talked to me about photography, and then he was gone. I couldn't help wondering what was going on in his head.

Was he, as I had first thought, just plain disgusted with me for what happened at Montauk? He was so friendly when he *did* talk to me, that I was beginning to suspect that wasn't the main issue. But then, I'd never know unless I got up the nerve to say something, and I was the world's biggest chicken. Maybe he just liked Candace better than me. Or maybe he had a girlfriend at home. Now there was an entirely new possibility that I had never even considered before. The frustration of not knowing was the worst of it. Then there was the problem of Jim. I knew he liked me, and I liked him, too. But definitely not in the same way. And how could I let him know that without hurting his feelings?

In addition to everything else, I realized I was changing a lot myself. Photography was becoming very important to me. When I sat at dinner with my family and found myself trying to figure out the best angle for taking a picture of them, I knew I wasn't the same Samantha Alexander who had boarded the plane for Saint Martin. Even if Keith never liked me as a girlfriend, at least he had turned me on to something terrific. I was sure I'd keep up with my photography at home, and I'd always think of Keith.

I wrote for pages in my diary. It took nearly an hour, and it felt really good. When I finally went back to the bedroom to go to sleep, I nearly tripped on one of Greg's paperbacks. I was sure it hadn't been there before. But why didn't he want me to know he had been up reading? I wondered as I hid my diary with its silver key in the bottom of my dresser. It wasn't as if I would tell Mom or Dad on him.

The next morning I got up and went to breakfast with my family for the first time in days. Keith hadn't said anything about meeting early at the pool, and I had just assumed he meant that our photo lessons were now over. Even though I wished they would go on forever, I didn't have the nerve to tell him. It seemed too much like something Candace might do to get attention. Anyway, snorkel lessons began at the pool at nine-thirty, so we all met there. It wasn't the same as a private, early get-together with Keith, but at least I was near him.

One of the Paradise Bay scuba instructors showed us how to use the masks, snorkels, and flippers, and we spent about half an hour swimming up and down the pool trying them out. It didn't seem very hard, and it was pretty boring because all we could see under the water were the lane markers painted on the pool's bottom.

Greg had come for lessons, too, even though he wasn't old enough to come on the snorkel trip. He picked up the technique just as quickly as anyone else, and I did have a moment of guilt for not offering to take him. But Jeremy Garson wasn't coming, I noticed. A year younger than Greg, he just sat on a lounger and watched us.

Learning to breathe with a big rubber snorkel jammed into my mouth did take a bit of practice. There were a couple of older people who gave up and climbed out of the pool.

Candace appeared to be having trouble, too, or maybe she was just enjoying the extra attention she was getting from our cute instructor.

By ten-thirty we were ready to take off for Sandy Island in the hotel's boats. Staff members waded a few feet out and loaded picnic hampers aboard one of the three Boston whalers while the rest of us climbed aboard with our towels and snorkel gear. As we six and another couple climbed into one boat, I saw Greg and Jeremy sitting by the shore watching us.

"Your brother looks so sad out there," Keith observed.

"Yes. You have to be twelve to come on this trip, and he's only nine. But I think he would have done just fine anyway. I feel sort of bad that I didn't offer to take him."

"Aren't you the nice older sister," Candace said sarcastically.

"I'm sure that the twelve-year-old cutoff is based on experience. He probably wouldn't have had the endurance," consoled Keith.

"Yeah," I agreed. I appreciated his words and wondered if he was aware of Candace's nasty comment. It was impossible to miss, but then, wasn't love supposed to be blind?

The boat cruised through the crystal-clear water and around a bend in the island, until the hotel was lost from sight. As I watched the ever-changing shoreline, I was able to forget about Greg, Candace, and Keith and get lost in the luxury of the soft, warm breeze, my mind lulled by the noise of the boat's motor. After a twenty-minute ride, Saint Martin looked very far away.

Finally two of the boats slowed to a stop while the third, containing the staff and picnic hampers, continued to cruise on ahead. We were anchoring in a quiet patch of water off Sandy Island facing a tiny spit of land.

The head instructor had briefed us thoroughly back at the pool, but he repeated his information about the route we would take around the island and what kinds of fish and coral we should expect to see. We would snorkel in three groups, each with a leader, for an hour. Then we would head for shore to eat the picnic lunch. He reminded us not to touch anything, no matter how innocent it looked.

Jumping off the boat with snorkel, mask, and flippers was not my favorite part of the expedition. My carefully arranged mask and snorkel didn't stay put. But I was able to readjust the equipment quickly. Our group leader asked if we were all ready, and then our journey began.

When all you've seen of the underwater world are the toys on the bottom of your bathtub, seeing a coral reef for the first time is a real experience. I was totally awed by the acres of miniature mountain ranges that existed below the water's surface. The exotically colored fish and bizarre plants were more spectacular than anything I'd ever imagined.

Jim and Keith were swimming just ahead of me, and we were gesturing to one another with exaggerated movements to point out the startling fish and plants. It was a funny way to communicate, but with snorkels in our mouths, talking was impossible.

Wearing flippers enabled me to swim a lot faster than I would normally. At one point I stuck my head out of the water to see how far we had come from the boat. You can imagine my surprise when I saw a lone figure, who looked like Candace, struggling with a snorkel and mask farther back in the water. Our group had all moved ahead, and so it was up to me to go back and help her out. She was still close enough to our anchored boat to climb aboard, I knew, but how disappointing it would be to miss all these sensational underwater sights.

It didn't take long for me to reach her. "Need any help?" I asked after I shifted my own mask up to my forehead and pulled the snorkel out of my mouth.

"I can't get this lousy snorkel on right, and

my mask is leaking, too. It's really a drag," she panted. She sounded truly defeated, and I felt bad for her.

"Let me see if I can get the snorkel on," I offered. "And maybe if I tighten the straps on the mask, it'll fit better."

She handed me the black rubber gear. "Something was bound to get messed up. Maybe I should just wait in the boat."

"The snorkel is hard to get used to," I told her as we treaded water. "But the reef is so beautiful, it would be a shame to miss it. Here, try this and see if it's better."

She cleared the mask as we had been shown and slipped it over her face, refitting the snorkel. "I'll stay near by in case you have problems," I assured her. "But let's catch up with the group. It's not hard to go fast with flippers."

Candace stuck her face in the water, and having determined that her mask was, in fact, no longer leaking, she took off.

I swam behind her to make sure she was OK, being careful to keep my face away from her moving flippers. We caught up to the group with no trouble and guess where she headed. Right to Keith!

Chapter Ten

Keith had been right about snorkeling. It wasn't all that hard to figure out, but it took a lot of energy. By the time our underwater expedition was over and we had waded ashore on Sandy Island, I was exhausted from having kicked for an hour with the heavy flippers on my feet. I knew now that Greg wouldn't have been able to keep up. As our group crawled onto the beach, other people complained, too, but miraculously, Candace was silent.

"That was hard work," panted Meryl.

"But terrific for those leg muscles," said Tom.

"I'm freezing," I chattered.

"Have you ever seen such fish!" asked Keith.

"Yeah, in my dentist's office," answered Jim, and most of us laughed.

"Hey," said Keith to the silent Candace, "you almost missed the trip." Everyone was very quiet, soaking up the warmth of the sun, and I waited to hear her answer.

"I had a little trouble getting started," she admitted.

"Good thing Samantha was there to help you out," he said. "We might have lost you altogether." His tone was light, inviting an easy, joking response.

But Candace had a mulish look on her face. "Yes," she finally admitted. "I guess so."

I couldn't believe it! I could understand that she might have been embarrassed, but how could she not have had the decency to thank me.

Gorgeous-looking sandwiches and salads had been laid out for us on a huge picnic table. We were so hungry, we practically inhaled our lunch. No one gave Candace's outrageous attitude a second thought. But as we sat around, talking about the beautiful sights we'd seen, I couldn't get her out of my mind. I knew I had done the right thing, despite my feelings for

Candace. After all, she could have been in serious trouble. But she hadn't even one word of thanks for me, and that hurt a lot. Anyway, Keith seemed to have noticed, which felt good.

After lunch we all stretched out on the white beach of our tiny, private island. I had been so chilled after snorkeling that I couldn't imagine ever feeling hot again, but the Caribbean sunshine was so powerful that it wasn't long before I was dying to get back in the water. We spent the rest of the afternoon playing in the water and building sand sculptures along the shore. At my suggestion, Keith, Tom, Jim, and I built an ocean liner in the sand around Meryl. We joked around and had a great time while Candace sat off by herself and sulked.

As the afternoon wore on, Candace began to complain of a pain in her leg. If she was expecting extra attention from any of us, Keith in particular, I was delighted to see that she didn't get it. In fact, Keith's only reaction was to give her one vaguely understanding word.

I dreaded the end of the afternoon, the end of my time with Keith. But there was nothing I could do to stop the clock, and eventually it was time to climb back into the boats and head for the hotel.

Candace hobbled down the beach and through the water on the arm of our cute instructor, yet it was impossible for me to work up any sympathy for her. She managed to commandeer the padded seat next to the driver for herself, while the rest of us sprawled on cushions around the edge of the boat. It was definitely the bumpy way to ride, but with Keith next to me, I hardly cared.

As the boat got close to the hotel, I began to plan seriously. There were only two days left of our vacation on Paradise Island, my time together with Keith. I couldn't just let him slip away from me. "Listen," I blurted out in a rush of gutsy emotion, "I still have a million more questions about photography. Do you think we could get together one more time for a lesson?"

Keith was silent for a moment as if considering a deep, important issue. "Sure," he answered finally. "Tomorrow morning would be the only time—except, well—" He stopped and thought for another moment. "Paul's been telling me I ought to check out the weekly open market in Marigot tomorrow morning. If you don't mind leaving by six, we could go together."

"That is definitely early—" I started.

"But it's something not many visitors get to see," he finished for me.

"How can I turn down a chance like that!" I said.

"You can't," he answered with a laugh.

When we reached the hotel, I walked back to the room floating on air. I was exhausted, but I was in ecstasy. Snorkeling had been incredible, but spending time with Keith had been even more wonderful.

And now we finally had a date to go shooting together, even if it was at six in the morning. Somehow, when I'd finally got up the nerve to ask for another lesson, I reflected, it was as if I had pressed the magic button. Keith had responded just the way I'd dreamed. What a fabulous day!

I showered and changed quickly so I wouldn't be late for dinner. I was combing my wet hair in the bathroom, fighting off exhaustion, when I heard Greg come in. "Hi," I called out.

"Well, if it isn't Samantha," he answered back. "How was the trip?" There was a peculiar, mischievous sound in his voice.

"It was terrific," I told him. He was stretched out on his bed, poring through one of his paperbacks.

"I'll bet," he answered.

"You know, Greg, I have to tell you that as nice as it was, it was also exhausting. I don't think I know any nine-year-old who could have made it."

"If you're trying to make excuses for not taking me, forget it, it's too late."

"What do you mean by that?"

"It's for me to know and you to find out," he said mysteriously.

At dinner I didn't want to talk too much about the snorkeling trip. There was no reason to make Greg feel any more resentful than he already did, but my parents were anxious to hear all about it.

"It was absolutely spectacular," I admitted to them while we were eating. "The reef looked like an exotic mountain range. It was so peaceful. I could have watched the fish for hours."

"I'm sorry I couldn't come," Dad said, "but I had to spend the morning working on tomorrow's big farewell bash."

"I can't believe the week has gone so fast," I said mournfully.

"We'll have to do it again sometime, without Globex," said Mom, "so your father can have a vacation, too."

"But it won't be the same without all the company kids," objected Greg. "They're so neat."

"It's nice to hear you say so, Greg," said Dad with a satisfied smile. "That makes all the work I've put into this worthwile."

After dinner I met up with Meryl, Tom, and Jim on the porch outside the dining room. The dark sky was lit by a million pinpoints of starlight, and the cool breeze made a rustling noise through the palm trees. So romantic, so peaceful. It would have been nice to sit there with Keith. But where was he? I wondered. He wasn't with Candace, I was sure, because I had just seen her minutes before, stone faced, in the dining room with the rest of her family. Meryl and Tom were sitting very close together whispering to each other. Then they got up and walked into the darkness holding hands.

"They seem so happy," Jim told me when they had gone. "I'm glad for my brother."

"Glad and sad," I told him. "Do you guys live anywhere near Meryl back home? Will they ever see each other again?"

"Actually," he told me, "Meryl lives about an hour from us, not too bad. But I'm mostly glad that Tom has gotten his self-confidence back. His girlfriend at home just broke up with him, and he's had a really rough time of it. Meryl's crazy about him, and I think that's helped him a lot. Besides, you know what they say about these vacation romances, don't you?"

"No, what?"

"That they're just flings."

"No, I hadn't realized."

"Don't take my brother's thing with Meryl so seriously."

"You're right," I said, trying to perk up my voice. But that's not at all what was on my mind. Jim had just given me yet another reminder that my friendship with Keith, as unromantic as it was, would soon be over forever.

But Jim had also helped me clear my mind of something else important. If Tom wasn't all that serious about his romance with Meryl, Jim, who had followed me around for days, certainly wasn't too committed to a romance with me. So when he put his arm around me as we sat in the warm dark Caribbean evening and tried to kiss me, I felt no guilt whatsoever when I stood up and moved away.

"I'm really tired from all that snorkeling," I told him. "I'm going to go back to the room."

"In other words, you're not interested in

taking a little tip from Tom and Meryl," he stated matter-of-factly.

"Not much," I confirmed. "Not that I don't like you. We've had a great time together. It's just that I seem to have a totally different idea from you about what I want from a friendship."

I walked back to the room with slow, deliberate steps. There was a lot on my mind that I needed to sort out, and I was sure that writing in my diary would help.

As I reached my door, I heard Keith call my name softly. He stepped out of the shadows, his eyes sparkling and his smile as friendly as ever.

"You scared me," I told him. "Where did you come from?"

"I'm just getting back from Paul's. I was anxious to see some new prints he was working on, so I rushed over there after Sandy Island."

"Were they fantastic?" I asked.

"Yes, I'm sorry you didn't come."

Not as sorry as I am, I thought. I asked Keith, "Aren't you exhausted?"

"I am, but I was about to take a walk along the beach before I turn in. I think I need to unwind. Want to come?"

"Sure. I'll just drop my shoes in here."

Turning the key in the door, I pushed it open to find Greg and Jeremy sitting on the bed playing cards.

"Oh, hi, guys," I said as I tossed in my shoes.

"Hi, Samantha," answered Greg, his tone as mischievous as it had been earlier.

As we headed down the path to the beach, I told Keith, "You know, I think my brother is still mad at me about the snorkel trip."

"It's tough to be too young to do stuff you think you're ready to do," Keith said.

Then he told me about Paul's new series of photographs, which had impressed him very much.

"Paul is something else," I said. "I bet you hate the idea of losing contact with him when this trip ends."

"Yes," he agreed. "This has been a special time, but I don't see it as the end of our friendship, you know. Paul spends quite a few months a year in New York City, and I intend to see him there. Besides, he's promised to correspond with me while he's here, so it's not as if I'm going to forget all about him."

"I'm glad," I said. "You've just restored my faith in friendship."

"What do you mean?" I told him about the

conversation I had just had with Jim. "Meryl and Tom will probably never see each other again, and from what Jim says, Tom doesn't even care!"

"Maybe Meryl feels the same way," Keith suggested.

"I don't know," I answered, shocked at the idea.

When we reached the beach, the moon had come up. With the water lapping on the shore and the soft sand beneath our feet, it was even more romantic than the veranda had been. And this time I had Keith by my side.

"How's Candace's leg?" he asked as we headed down toward the water. It sounded like he really cared.

How could he even bring up such a disgusting subject at a time like this? Was Candace really on his mind?

"I wouldn't know," I answered. "She doesn't confide in me much. In fact, she doesn't even talk to me, as you may have noticed."

"I think I've hit a raw nerve," he said. "She's been pretty rotten to you, hasn't she?"

"You're not kidding. She may be a winner at Ping-Pong, but she's a real loser in my book. You know, I really went out of my way to help her this morning, not that I'm expecting a medal or anything, but she never even thanked me. In fact, she's been acting as if I did something wrong. Can you believe it?"

Suddenly I was struck with an incredible thought. Had Candace faked her trouble in the beginning so Keith would come to her rescue? It was scary to think she would have played such a dangerous game to get his attention, especially since she seemed so genuinely distressed when I reached her.

"Keith, I have to tell you something I just thought of," I said slowly, wondering how he would respond to my idea. "I think Candace expected you to swim over and save her. And I think she's furious because I did instead."

Keith was silent for a moment, digesting what I had said. Then he started to laugh. He laughed so hard that I had to start laughing, too. "So *that's* it!" He shook his head. "When *is* that girl going to figure out that she's just not my type?"

Chapter Eleven

So Candace Vale was not Keith's type. That was the best news I had had. I never thought she was, of course, but it was a relief to hear it from Keith himself.

We walked along the cool sand joking about how Candace had coerced Keith into doing things. "I was always on my way to or from Paul's," he explained. "So it was no big deal to give her a ride. And as for Ping-Pong, she *is* awfully good."

"A champ," I agreed.

"She could be fun sometimes," he went on, and I could feel the jealousy well up inside of me. "But it wasn't until I saw how she treated you that I realized she just wasn't a very nice person."

"Understatement of the year."

"Why didn't you ever give her a taste of her own medicine?"

"I'm not sure what I could have done," I admitted. "Besides, that's just not my style." As soon as I said it, I stopped. Keith must have thought that was pretty funny coming from me, the person who ran off in Montauk and hid behind a locked door. But he didn't say anything, and neither did I.

"She won't have Samantha Alexander to kick around much longer, will she?" he said as if this reminder would cheer me up.

"That's not exactly the kind of solution I had in mind. I really love it here, and I'm definitely not ready to go home."

"I know, but there's nothing to be done for the moment, so I suggest you stop worrying and enjoy what's left of our trip. Are you still planning to join me for the market tomorrow morning?"

"I wouldn't miss it for the world."

Then something fantastic happened. As we walked back to the hotel, I felt Keith put his arm around my shoulder. He was so relaxed, so nonchalant, as if it were the usual way we walked together.

As for me, I was so totally surprised, I began to tremble. Can you believe it! Here, at the most momentous moment of my life, I was turning into a quivering mass of Jell-O. If the beach in front of us had parted at that moment, I would gladly have jumped into the chasm to hide my embarrassment.

This was the time to say something about Montauk, I knew, but I soon discovered that being so close to Keith had left me speechless as well as everything else. The only thing I could do was work on calming myself down, and fast. It wasn't easy, but taking a couple of long, deep breaths helped. Then, when I felt in control, more or less, I wrapped my arm around Keith's waist, where it seemed to fit perfectly.

"I'm bringing along my last six rolls of film tomorrow," he said. "And you're welcome to as much as you need."

"Thanks, but I have two rolls left. Dad did tell me that most people use Kodacolor, which has been long gone."

"There aren't many of us weirdos around who just use black and white," he said, giving my shoulder a gentle squeeze.

It was odd, to say the least, to have a perfectly normal, easygoing conversation about photography as we walked so close. After all, if you were as good friends with a guy as I was with Keith, wouldn't it feel perfectly normal to walk along a moonlit Caribbean beach snuggled up close to each other?

Ha! Of course not. But did I mean anything special to him? At that moment I really didn't want to know. I was too happy.

We walked along the shore, each lost in silent thoughts, until it was time to turn up to the hotel. And it was the most natural thing in the world when he kissed me. He tasted warm and sweet. I closed my eyes and kissed him back, wishing the moment would last forever.

"Mmm," he said dreamily when we stopped for air. "I've never kissed a photographer before."

"What does that mean?"

"I guess I just don't know any other girl photographers."

"I can't believe that!"

"Or maybe I just don't know any that I've wanted to kiss." He walked me to the door of my room, and we kissed again. It felt even better than the first time. "I'll meet you in the front lobby at six tomorrow morning. Think you can make it?"

"I'll set my alarm," I assured him. After a last, brief kiss, he turned and was gone.

My senses were completely bonkers as I pushed open the door to my room. I must have been the happiest person in all of Saint Martin, not to mention the most exhausted and most confused. I threw myself down on my bed for just a moment. I wanted to think things over as carefully as I could. Was I about to have my heart broken? I wondered. We'd be leaving so soon. Would my romance with Keith be over before it even started?

It was really early, just a little after ten. Greg wasn't even in yet. I knew I had to change out of my clothes and get washed. Besides, I had the most important news in the world, and I had to write it all down in my diary. Except, I couldn't will myself to stand up—I couldn't even will myself to move. The next thing I knew, it was morning.

Actually, when I woke up I assumed I had dozed off for a few minutes. I was still wearing my sun dress, which was a wrinkled disaster. Greg was now snoring peacefully in his own bed.

But the clock next to my bed said 5:35 A.M.

Jumping up, I rushed into the bathroom to get washed. By three minutes of six, I was standing in the lobby, camera over my shoulder, waiting for Keith.

He arrived only moments later, looking only half awake. "I almost didn't make it," he confessed. "I slept right through the alarm. Jeremy finally woke me up to shut it off."

"Well, I fell asleep last night before I even could set my alarm. By some miracle, I woke up about half an hour ago."

"What a pair of devoted photographers we are!" he said, reaching out to squeeze my hand. Memories of the night before came flooding back to me. At least I thought they were memories. They could have been dreams.

We walked out to the parking lot. The sun was starting to rise, the sky was pearly gray. The air still had an early morning chill, which made me clasp my hands to my arms to keep warm as Keith drove the open car on to the road.

"I can't believe we're doing this," I said. "I have a funny, fuzzy feeling in my head."

"It does seem like unnecessary torture, but I think we'll be glad in the end."

"Can you drive a little more carefully?" I

complained. "All those bumps in the road are waking me up."

"Yeah, me, too."

The time I had been to Marigot, two days earlier, had been in the middle of the afternoon. The road had been lined with cars, and the town had been humming with the activity of vacationers looking for exotic bargains. But Marigot at six-fifteen in the morning was a totally different place. The sidewalks were deserted. Decorative metal gates, drawn across shop fronts, made them look like they were sleeping as deeply as I should have been.

Keith parked the car, and we walked out to the pier where I had been with Jim. Now, with Keith by my side, it was a dream come true, a moment I would remember forever. As we rounded the corner and the pier came into sight, I felt myself snap to attention. My head was still muddled, but I was able to feel the excitement and to be intrigued by the hectic picture in front of me.

Hundreds of people had gathered together to buy and sell brightly colored fruits, vegetables, and fish from hastily assembled tables and crates. I couldn't even identify half the things they were selling. There were even small palm trees, their roots wrapped in crude fabric, offered for sale. The dock was lined with wooden freight boats, which were being unloaded by many hardworking people.

"This is really something," I whispered to Keith. "But do you feel as out of place as I do?"

"I feel like a visitor, yes, but I don't feel especially uncomfortable, if that's what you mean. The first few times I went places to photograph people, I did feel like a real intruder. When people see cameras, they freeze up sometimes."

"So what do you do?"

"It all depends. Sometimes I ask permission to take a picture, sometimes I don't. And I never continue with a shot if it seems to be bothering someone. You have to respect a person's right to privacy."

"That probably doesn't leave too many people to photograph," I guessed.

"You'd be surprised. Some people actually want you to take their pictures, and that can be a problem, too." He laughed. "Anyway, I have a neat technique that I can recommend for taking pictures in a crowd that won't annoy anyone. Focus for a middle range, hold the camera over your head, and shoot as you turn in a circle."

"Sounds crazy," I told him.

"You find a lot of surprises in the pictures."

"Surprises?"

"Yes, you get some interesting stuff that you might not have captured otherwise. But there's also a lot of frustration involved," he admitted. "Like shots that could have been great if they had been in focus."

"I know all about that," I said. "I think I'll stick to boats."

"The boats down here are pretty neat," he admitted. "But don't get caught in a rut. Try to keep yourself open and see how it goes."

"I think I'll start right here with this great-looking boat," I told him. "But I promise I'll work on other subjects, too."

"Good," he approved. "Let's try to keep tabs on each other, but if we get lost, I'll meet you back at the car at seven-thirty."

"Fine," I answered as I began to focus on the boat that was piled high with pinkish, banana-shaped fruit. I clicked off five or six shots before I turned around to find Keith. It was easy to spot him in the crowd. He was talking to a tall black woman with a flowered scarf tied around her head. In front of her was a tray of large, bright fish like some I had seen snorkeling. It looked like he had asked permission to photograph her. I watched, fascinated, as she stood behind her wares while Keith worked with his camera.

I admired the way Keith was able to deal with strangers. Remembering what he had just suggested about taking pictures in a crowd, I decided to try using his random technique, since I knew I wasn't ready to deal with people on a one-to-one basis.

Choosing a middle focus and a good place to stand, I began to shoot off pictures, turning slightly after each shutter click. It was a totally new and different approach for me, and it was fun.

The marketplace was so active, so ever changing, and so different from anywhere I had ever been before that I knew, even if they were mostly out of focus, the pictures would be interesting to me. And that's what gave me the energy to continue.

I have to admit that I did as much just plain looking and listening as I did picture taking. Watching people bargain with one another was fascinating to me, even though I couldn't understand all of what they were saying. The island accent was sometimes hard to understand.

When it was time to meet Keith, I had finished one and a half rolls of film. He was leaning against his car, reloading his camera. "How did it go?" he asked, concentrating on the film.

"It's hard to say," I told him. "But I'm totally in love with this place. I want to stay forever."

"Me, too," he agreed, looking away from what he was doing to stare into my eyes. "Hey, let's not get too sad. Want to have some breakfast? That little café on the corner looks like it's getting ready to open."

We sat at a tiny table on the sidewalk outside the café so we could still see the hectic marketplace. We were the only customers, and we ordered croissants and hot chocolate, which the waiter delivered to us on a brass-edged tray.

"I used your method of taking pictures in the crowd, but I really admire the way you're able to deal with complete strangers," I told him as we spread jam on our croissants. "You make it look so easy. I'm always afraid somebody is going to laugh at me or something."

"It was hard at first," he admitted. "But generally I've found that people can be pretty friendly. And it's been worth the effort because I've met some fascinating people and learned a lot of amazing things. Getting into photography has meant a lot more to me than just taking pictures. It's meant learning about myself, too."

I took a deep breath. "I've never been very good at direct confrontation," I confessed, thinking about Montauk.

"Take it from me, if you want something badly enough, you can figure out a way to get it. I used to be the shyest kid in the world." He bit into his croissant as if to emphasize his point.

"I can't believe it! You've always seemed so outgoing and straightforward."

"You didn't know me a couple years ago."

Sure I did, I said to myself, wondering if I should say it aloud. Had the moment come for me to discuss Montauk with Keith? Could I do it? Keith continued on about himself, and his voice was so charged with emotion that my own problems faded for the moment.

"Back then it was truly painful for me to talk to anyone except my best friend. Going to school was torture. You see, I was a freshman at the same school my father had attended. He had been a big-time athlete when he was a kid, and he expected me to be a superstar, too. But I was never especially good at sports, nor was I the student government type. I just kind of blended into the woodwork where I was very happy to hide. "Here," he said, passing me a little pottery pitcher. "Hot chocolate is best with a little cream in it." I poured the cream and stirred my chocolate.

"So what happened?"

"I got into photography."

"How did that help?"

"I started taking pictures of people at school. The more I took pictures of them, the more I talked to them, and the more I realized that they had other things to say besides who scored the winning touchdown or got the most votes in the student election. Then I was able to put my life in better perspective."

"Like what?" I dipped the end of my croissant into my hot chocolate and took a bite.

"Like it's real nice that Dad was a superjock and class president, but it didn't mean I was a failure if I was into something else. The trouble is, even though I'm happy with what I'm doing and excited that I could have a great future in it, Dad is still determined to make me into himself." Keith looked away, but I could tell this was very painful for him to talk about.

"But he seems so proud of you. At least, that's the impression I get from my father."

"To him, taking pictures is a fine hobby, but he won't be happy unless I go to business school and get involved with the selling end of photography." Keith sounded really discouraged.

"But he can't make you do what you don't want to, can he?"

"No, but he can prevent me from doing what I want to do." He stared into my eyes.

"And what's that?"

"I want to go to a really good photography college, like Rochester Institute, where I can study with the best teachers in the world."

"How are you going to work that out?"

"What I've decided is, I've got to be the best that I can possibly be. That's one reason why I spent so much time with Paul while we were here. I can't believe how much he's taught me in six days!" Keith popped the last of his croissant into his mouth and licked his fingers with an assured air.

"It sounds like you're definitely on the right track."

"If I can only win the Globex photo contest. The judges are big photography dealers, and I know their opinions will go a long way to impress Dad."

"Your father's not blind to how hard you're working."

"True, but he's a tough man to sway once his mind is made up."

"It doesn't sound like you're ready to give up on him, though."

"Like I said, some things are worth fighting for." He had a very determined look on his face, and I could tell that he really meant what he was saying.

"Keith," I started slowly, "I don't know whether you know how much your photography lessons have meant to me. Thank you for being so patient."

"No problem," he said, brushing it off. "I'm glad that you've gotten into it. Truthfully, when your father asked me to do it, I never thought you'd turn out to be so—well, motivated, so serious. But I was very pleasantly surprised." He motioned to the waiter for the check. "This is my treat," he said as he paid the bill.

"Thanks."

"But really, I like to teach photography for purely selfish reasons," he confessed. "When I explain something, I end up understanding it better myself." I smiled at him, relieved to know, finally, why he had been such a willing teacher. He really just liked doing it! "Anyway, it's great to have a new friend to share photography with. I just hope you'll take pictures when you get home, that this hasn't been a brief fling."

"Oh, no," I denied. "I'm planning to join the photography club when I get back."

"That's a good start."

"But I'm having trouble believing that tonight is our last night. Tomorrow I'll be back in the freezing cold!" I looked out at the busy tropical market. North Hollow seemed a million years away.

"Then, I move that we don't think about it," he said, abruptly pushing his chair away from the table and standing up. "Let's just get ourselves out on the beach and soak up all the rays we can."

He paid for our breakfast, and we walked back to the car arm in arm. While the motor was warming up, Keith took my hand, leaned over, and gave me a long, delicious kiss.

"That was to seal our bargain," he explained. "We've sworn to ignore reality for just a few hours longer."

"No problem." I laughed, and my spirits soared.

Chapter Twelve

I should have realized that things were not going to be as easy as they seemed. It was fun to pretend with Keith that we could ignore the inevitable. But it was totally unrealistic.

For one thing, I wasn't going to be at peace with myself until I had discussed Montauk with him. Like Keith, I knew I had learned a lot during our vacation, and one thing I knew more clearly than ever was that I had to apologize to him no matter what it did to our friendship. Or was it a romance?

There was something else I knew now, too. Keith was a real person, not just a cute face, and I was crazy about him. But this feeling had not made me blind to his faults. He was a whiz at dealing with people—as long as he was holding his camera. Then he was relaxed and open. But he was as afraid of a direct confrontation with me as I was with him.

Having had our revealing, soul-searching discussion about photography and his father made me think the moment was right to bring up Montauk. During the car ride home from Marigot, I started to mention it a few times, but Keith never let me get it out. He kept changing the subject. He seemed almost more afraid of it than I was!

When we got back to the hotel, we put our equipment away and headed for the beach were there was a big volleyball game in progress. Meryl, Tom, Jim, and Candace were all playing, and we were immediately invited into the game.

Jumping around in the hot sun was the last thing I wanted to do, so I just sat under a palm tree. But Keith joined in, taking Candace's place on the team. "Saved at last," she told him, hobbling slightly. As the game continued, she sat down next to me on the sand. She was the last person in the world I felt like talking to. "Keith got here just in time," she said, wiping her sweaty brow. Her tone was friendlier than I had ever heard it. "Where have you guys been?"

"Down in Marigot," I answered, but I offered no more information.

"So early? Nothing opens until eleven."

"We went to photograph the Saturday market. It opens at six." I guess my monotone voice had put her off because Candace was silent for a few minutes as we watched the volleyball game.

"Actually, Samantha," she said finally, "I wanted to thank you for helping me out yesterday." I could tell by her voice that this was a hard thing for her to do.

"You're welcome, Candace," I responded, but I was not too gracious. I mean, really, did she expect me to jump up and down just because she was getting around to saying thank you?

"I also want to apologize for the way I acted," she continued, her voice even more humble. "It was kind of embarrassing for me to need your help."

"Maybe if Keith had helped it wouldn't have been so bad," I offered.

"Somehow, I *did* imagine myself being rescued by someone like Keith," she affirmed stiffly.

"Sorry to have upset your plans."

"Well, that's why I wanted to apologize. I'm really thankful that you got there when you did. I really did need some help, but I was too self-conscious to admit it."

"Better late than never."

"Yeah," she said. Well, Candace was definitely trying hard, I'd say that for her. But I didn't see any reason to get all buddy-buddy with her so suddenly. "Also, I wanted to say that I think you're really good at Ping-Pong. You gave me quite a battle at the tournament."

"But you were just a bit better, weren't you?"

"Maybe yes, maybe no. Let's just say I was having a good night. Anyway, since we're all going home tomorrow, I wanted to try to make peace with you."

"I can't imagine why."

"I've never apologized like this before to anyone," she confessed. "It's just that Jim and I were talking about you this morning, and I came away feeling like maybe we should be friends."

"Great," I answered with little enthusiasm,

but then I thought a moment and continued in a different tone. "I'm sorry if I'm being sarcastic, but you really made me mad a lot of times. On the other hand, I know how hard it is to apologize, and that counts for a lot."

"You do?" She sounded surprised.

"If you only knew! I've owed someone an apology for a long time, and I just can't get myself to do it."

"You—whom everybody likes. That seems impossible."

"Well, it's true. All I can say, Candace, is thank you. You have just given me the courage to try again." I was smiling now, and she smiled back at me. It was almost as if we really were friends.

When the volleyball game was over, we all decided to get sandwiches and lemonade from the snack bar, instead of wasting time going to the dining room. As Keith sat next to me in the sand munching on his sandwich, I kept remembering the way he had kissed me. It had felt as if it really meant something special to him. But then he'd refused to talk about anything serious in our relationship. Was he, like my other vacation friends, just interested in the moment? Was it wrong for me to keep hoping for something more?

As I walked back to the room later that afternoon to shower and change, I resolved to get things straightened out once and for all that night at the farewell barbeque. If Candace, snob of the world, could work up the nerve to apologize to me, certainly I could apologize to Keith. And then maybe I'd bring the discussion around to something more romantic. So, whether or not I ended up with a broken heart, at least my conscience would be clear.

Everything might have been fine, if it hadn't been for Greg's little surprise. "I thought you'd never get back," he said with a scowl when I pushed open the door to our room.

"It's so nice to be wanted," I answered, pretending to misinterpret his unfriendly tone.

"I didn't want to miss your face when you figured out my great joke."

"Oh, what's that?"

"It's about your diary."

"What about it?"

"You couldn't write in it last night."

"I know. I fell asleep."

"I thought so. Well, you won't be able to write in it tonight, either."

"Why not?"

"It's not here."

"Where is it?"

"That's for me to know and you to find out."

"Gregory!" I jumped at him and grabbed his wrists. "Where is it?"

"I gave it to Keith Garson, or at least Jeremy did."

"What do you mean?" I shrieked. Letting go of his wrists, I backed away, shocked.

"You were really mean to me," he whined. "So I decided to get back at you. I took your diary out of its hiding place. I knew where it was all along. And I gave it to Jeremy to give to Keith. Of course, I read it first. That's how I decided on Keith, instead of Jim."

"When?" I demanded.

"This morning, after breakfast."

My mind was working fast. So Keith had not seen it before our trip to the market. And he probably hadn't seen it when he dropped his camera off afterward. But he was probably sitting in his room reading it at that very moment.

"Greg, how could you!" I wailed, clenching my fists.

"It was easy, really. Now you'll think twice before you say you won't let me come on a trip with you."

"And now, I'll never let you come *anywhere* with me. I told you yesterday that the snorkeling would have been too tiring for you, and I meant it."

"Pooh" was all he said, and then he left the room.

I was so furious and frustrated that I threw myself down on my bed and hid my face in my pillow. Thinking about all the soul-searching, private thoughts I had written in my diary, I knew I would die of embarrassment before I could ever look Keith in the face again. My brave resolve of the afternoon vanished like a bubble, leaving me feeling broken and lifeless. My nose and eyes burned, and soon my pillow was soaked through with tears. Gradually I escaped my sorrow in a deep sleep.

I might have missed the barbeque altogether—I would have been glad to, in fact—if I hadn't been awakened by a loud knocking on the door. Who could it be? Not Keith, I hoped, anyone but Keith. It turned out to be my mother, and I realized that, despite what had happened, I was pretty disappointed that it wasn't Keith.

"Samantha, we were getting worried about you, and Greg thought you'd be here," she said as she walked in. She looked pretty in her light blue party dress. "Good heavens, you're still in your bathing suit. Are you feeling OK?

Did you have too much sun?" It had gotten dark and she switched on the lamp.

"I guess I fell asleep," I told her, squinting and rubbing my eyes. "I got up at five-thirty this morning, so I must have been more tired than I thought."

"Let me look at you," she said, gently taking my shoulders and staring at my face. "No, it's something else, isn't it," she said quietly. "You've been crying, Sam."

I nodded my head up and down.

"Want to tell me about it?" Mom had always been a good listener.

"Really, Mom, it's so complicated, I don't even know where to start." I hid my face and felt the tears come again.

"I've got all night," she assured me.

"What about Dad's party?"

"This seems more important. The party can take care of itself."

"Well, if you're sure," I said.

"Sure, I'm sure."

So she sat down next to me on my bed while I started from the beginning of my story, at Montauk, and haltingly told her all the things that had been going on between Keith and me since then.

"And I really thought I was going to get it all

worked out once and for all, when Greg had to come along and be such a total creep. I just can't believe him," I finished, before breaking into quiet sobs again.

"Greg certainly went out of bounds this time," Mom agreed. "And I'll have to decide the best way to deal with him."

"Punishing Greg is not going to help me one little bit," I objected. "That's not why I told you all this stuff."

"You're upset because of the embarrassment you feel."

I just cried all the harder.

"I can't make that go away," she said sadly. "No matter how much I wish I could."

"I know, Mom, but I'm glad I told you, anyway."

"So what do you want to do now?" she asked. "Hide out here or come say goodbye to everyone?"

"You mean I have a choice?"

"Of course."

"Then, I'll definitely stay here."

"If that's what you want, but I think you'll feel better if you face Keith, despite what Greg did. This may be your last chance for quite a while to clear your conscience. I'd hate to see this thing haunt you for a long time."

"It seems like the whole world is better than I am at facing stuff like this," I said, shaking my head. "I'd rather stay here."

"Your time will come," said Mom, kissing me on the top of my head, and she went back to the party.

I showered, changed into a nightgown, and climbed into bed with one of the romances I had brought from home but hadn't gotten to read since the beginning of the trip. It seemed so long ago.

But my concentration was nonexistent, and every time I read a page my thoughts drifted back to Keith. Had he finished reading my diary? Did he hate me now that he knew my innermost thoughts? Would he come to the room to tell me off? Would I ever know another boy like Keith? Suddenly there was a knock on the door, and I leaped to answer it. Too late I realized that I was wearing my eight-hundred-year-old nightgown.

But when I opened the door, it was only Meryl. "Samantha, we missed you at the barbeque. Come join us at Splashes," she said, "for our own farewell party."

"If you really want to know, I don't especially want to see Keith," I admitted.

"What! I thought you guys got all that

worked out. Well, not to worry, he just took off for his friend Paul's house. He said to tell you he'd see you in the morning at the pool before breakfast."

"Ah, reprieve," I said as I ran to the closet to pull out a sun dress. After swearing Meryl to secrecy, I told her what Greg had done.

"I'd murder him if I were you," she swore.

"And I'd go to jail for the rest of my life."

"Then how about slow torture?"

"Better," I agreed. "But in the meantime, how am I ever going to face Keith again? How can I meet him at the pool tomorrow?"

"What's in the diary, anyway?"

"It's just the whole story about Keith way back from the beginning."

"Is there a lot of dirt about other boys, or anything interesting like that?"

"Not much," I admitted. "I've never felt about anyone the way I feel about Keith."

"So what's the big deal?"

"I don't know how he feels about me!"

"And you'll never know unless you meet him. Sometimes, Samantha, you seem incredibly dense."

Meryl and I went to meet Tom, Jim, and Candace at Splashes. As we all sat around exchanging addresses on scraps of paper, I couldn't help but marvel at how this table of people, strangers just a week ago, had become such good friends in so short a time. We had all had such fun together. Even Candace, who had been a royal pain, had had her moment of being a reasonable human being.

It made me sad to think that it would all be over soon, that the next night I'd be home in my own house. Was I the only one feeling this way? I wondered. Keith had suggested we ignore the inevitable, and it looked like that's exactly what he was doing. Watching my friends around the table, it seemed like they were unaffected, too. But I knew that underneath their laughter and jokes, they were sad about leaving, too.

"I propose a toast to The Blizzard," announced Tom.

"What blizzard?" asked Candace.

"The one I just invented that will close down all the airports in the Northeast tomorrow."

"I'll drink to that," I agreed, holding up my lemonade.

"Here, here!" Jim cheered. Somehow, it was reassuring to know I wasn't the only one feeling depressed. But right after Tom's spirited toast, we all fell into a gloomy silence.

"I hate goodbyes," Jim said finally.

"Me, too," agreed his brother.

"This is not goodbye forever," Meryl pointed out, "just goodbye for now."

"Right," agreed Tom, squeezing her shoulder and looking very much like he meant it. I was happy for them, happy that their friendship and romance would continue on in some way after all. But I couldn't help being sad for myself and Keith. For us, I was afraid, it was really going to be goodbye forever.

Chapter Thirteen

Greg handed me my diary when I got back to the room.

"So soon?" I asked in my nastiest voice.

"He's a fast reader" was all Greg would say. I guessed by the sour look on his face that Mom really had talked to him.

I was relieved to have my diary back, but I definitely got the creeps when I thought about Keith, and Greg, and maybe even Jeremy reading all my innermost secrets. In fact, I couldn't imagine that I'd ever be able to write in it again. I even considered throwing it into the wastepaper basket and leaving it behind in Saint Martin, that's how upset I was. In the end I just tossed it into my suitcase as I started to pack.

"Mom said I should apologize," Greg offered as he lay on his own bed, staring at the ceiling.

"Don't bother if you don't mean it," I told him. "But don't think this is the end of it," I threatened.

As I walked to the pool to meet Keith the next morning, I still didn't know what I was going to say to him. I noticed with sadness that a few of the hotel vans were pulling off in the distance. For some, the unavoidable trip back to winter had begun already. My own flight wasn't until three o'clock in the afternoon.

Throwing myself into a lounge chair to wait, I was a nervous wreck. Keith had always been so punctual. So when he hadn't shown up by eight-thirty, I finally had to acknowledge that he wasn't coming. He'd run away from me, just as I'd run away from him in Montauk. It was the perfect way to get back at me!

Wandering into the dining room, I was near tears. I knew I had done something horrible to Keith, but that was such a long time ago. I'd always meant to apologize. He must have known that from reading my diary. It just didn't seem right. Keith was too nice to be so mean.

I was headed for my family's table when Meryl tapped me on the shoulder. "Hey, come sit with me for the last morning," she said.

"Great." I was happy to see her and delighted not to have to look at Greg. The urge to strangle him was still strong.

"Where's Tom?" I asked as soon as we had sat down.

"Gone," she said mournfully.

"What do you mean? I thought their flight was right before lunch."

"It *was*—until six o'clock this morning, when the charter company called to say it was leaving at nine-thirty. Can you imagine! Tom woke me up at six-thirty to say goodbye. My mother was furious."

"I wonder if the Garsons were on that flight," I said quietly.

"Could be. I think Candace might have been, too."

"I never got to say goodbye to Keith." I explained how I had waited for him at the pool and how I had worried that this was his way of getting back at me.

"Well, maybe he was on that flight," she mused. "Whatever happened with your diary?"

"Greg gave it back last night. Oh, I can't stand this," I complained, clutching my fists. "I wish I had never come on this trip!"

"Really?" She sounded shocked.

"Well, almost. I guess I just wish things had ended differently."

Meryl and I spent the morning wandering around the hotel for a final time. I finished up the roll of film in Keith's camera, and every time I clicked off a shot, I thought of him.

"I can't believe he didn't say goodbye," I said to Meryl. "I mean, I've still got his camera and all."

"Maybe he left you a note," she suggested.

"How could he have done that?"

"I don't know. Maybe there's something at the front desk."

I practically flew over to the main desk, Meryl following. Sure enough, the clerk pulled out a Paradise Bay envelope with my name scrawled on the outside. I ripped it open and pulled out the paper. The message inside was equally scribbled:

Samantha—our flight was rescheduled, and we had to leave early. Sorry not to say goodbye in person. I'll be in touch.

Keith

P.S. Please explain what happened to Paul when he stops by.

My eyes started to sting, and I was afraid I might cry.

"Do you feel any better now?" Meryl asked when I showed it to her.

"At least I know he wasn't being mean, not that I ever really believed he was." I tried to laugh, but I couldn't do a very convincing job. "But it's more than that. I like Keith more than any boy I've ever met before. I thought maybe he liked me a lot, too. But that was before he read my diary."

"He doesn't sound mad in his note," she observed.

"No, but he sounds the way he always has—nice and friendly. You'd think if he really cared he would have signed 'love' at the end."

"Oh, Samantha," she groaned and threw up her hands.

I stood and reread Keith's note about a million times while Meryl went over to the hotel boutique to buy a Paradise Bay tote bag. I finally had to admit that there was, in fact, nothing written between the lines.

I looked up to discover Paul Bostwick coming toward me carrying a canvas portfolio.

"Samantha," he greeted me, "I'm glad I found you. I've got the contact sheets of the negatives you and Keith developed." He pulled the sheets and an envelope of negatives from his case. "I think you'll be very pleased with some of your pictures. There's one delightful series of a blue heron, an all too rare bird." They were the pictures I had taken at the swamp, and he was pointing to a few tiny rectangles that he had circled with a red grease pencil. "These two look especially good," he told me.

I squinted at the tiny images, thrilled with what I saw. "Wow, I'd nearly forgotten all about these. Thanks a million."

"No problem. I told Keith I'd drop them by this morning. I know you're all leaving today, and I wanted to say goodbye."

I explained how Keith and a lot of other people had had to catch an early-morning flight.

"That's too bad," he said when I was finished. "But I've got Keith's number in New York, and I'll give him a call next month when I come up."

We said our goodbyes, shook hands, and Paul kissed me on the cheek. I was amazed at how close I felt to him after such a short time. "I hope you'll keep up with your photography," he told me. "I look forward to seeing your work next time we meet."

Meryl arrived with her tote bag, and we headed down to the beach for our last few hours of hot sun.

"It's weird with everyone gone," she said as we lay on our loungers. "I even miss Candace, can you believe it?"

The morning drifted away, and all too soon we were in a Paradise Bay van heading for the airport. Meryl and I sat next to each other on the plane back to New York, and we entertained each other thinking up spectacular places for the next Globex family vacation.

"How about mountain climbing in the Alps?" she suggested.

"Too cold. How about visiting the pyramids in Egypt?"

"Too hot. How about a vacation on the cool shores of sunny Saint Martin?"

"Just right," I agreed.

Chapter Fourteen

Adjusting to life back home in North Hollow was not easy. For one thing, the temperature was about twenty-two degrees. Feeling my nose stinging with cold as I walked home from school that first day, I tried to imagine I was back on the warm beach with Keith.

I did have Keith's camera, and for a few days I held on to it as if it were my most prized possession. I threw myself into picture taking as if it were a secret link to Keith. And I found a good camera shop on Main Street where I could have my film developed and printed. I have to admit, it was painful when I got back the pictures from Saint Martin. Seeing the shots of the open market, not to mention the close-ups of Keith sitting by the pool, made me happy and sad all over again.

One night, a few days after we got back, Dad remembered about Keith's equipment. "Do you still have the Garson boy's camera?" he asked.

"Yes," I admitted. "He left before I could return it."

"Hmm," he considered. "Why don't you pack it up, and I'll give it to Dave in the office."

"But I'm still using it," I objected.

"I'll bring you one of your own."

So I kissed Keith's camera goodbye, and Dad brought me a new one. It was identical to the other, but it just wasn't the same.

With the camera gone, I found myself looking at my Saint Martin contact sheets over and over again. Some of the pictures looked pretty good to me, and I knew that Paul Bostwick had liked some of my shots. I picked two and had them printed at the camera store. Then I sealed them into a manila envelope with my name and a cardboard sheet for stiffening. Looking up the address of Dad's office in the phone book, I mailed them off to the Globex photography contest without a word to anyone. If I didn't win anything, no one would ever have to know I'd entered.

A few days later when I got home from school, there was a letter waiting for me on the hall table, written in a familiar scrawl. Out of the corner of my eye, I saw my mother watching from the living room as I ripped open the envelope and devoured every word.

Dear Samantha,

Sorry not to have written sooner but I've been busy developing all the Saint Martin film since we got back. I've got a couple of shots from the market that look really good, and I've been working day and night to make perfect prints. Are you going to enter? Thanks for returning my camera. I hope you got one to replace it. It's hard being home, isn't it? Keep in touch.

Keith

"I see you've heard from Keith," observed Mom, coming in from the hall. "How are things?" She was trying hard to sound nonchalant, but I knew she realized how much I cared.

"Well," I told her, "he's as nice as ever."

She patted me on the shoulder. "Maybe he's smarter than you think," she said and disappeared.

I read the letter over and over again. Fighting the urge to pour my heart out to him, I wrote a return letter than was just as brief as his. When it was done, I fished out my diary, which I hadn't touched since my wretched little brother gave it back, and wrote for pages. Then I found a new hiding place for it in my closet.

After about a week, I found myself racing home from school every day, hoping for a letter from Keith. Finally I decided I had to put Keith out of my mind totally and completely, or else I would turn into a zombie. So every time I found myself drifting into a daydream about Paradise Bay or wondering why he hadn't written, I'd force myself to get busy with something else. It worked—most of the time. For one thing, I went to the monthly meeting of the North Hollow Camera Club, which was kind of fun. I signed up for darkroom time and got one of the other kids to refresh me on developing procedures.

Then one day as I was pushing my bangs out of my eyes, I looked in the mirror and noticed that my hair had actually grown.

Studying myself at all angles, I tried to imagine having long hair. You'll never guess what I did next. I made an appointment to have it trimmed again! I had come to really like the new me.

Nearly a month went by, and I got another letter from Keith. It was an interesting, cheerful letter. If he had only signed it "Love, Keith," it would have been a perfect letter. But he hadn't.

Keith had made no mention of my diary in either of his letters, and finally I could no longer stand the suspense. Confronting him in writing would be easier than doing it in person, I decided, so I ran up to my room and wrote a heartrending letter that went on for three pages. But when I reread it, I ripped it into a million pieces and started again. After all, no matter how much I wanted to explain to Keith, I didn't want to overwhelm him with mush. The new letter was in the same short, chatty style Keith had used.

Dear Keith,

It sounds like you're keeping really busy in the darkroom. I know you'll be a winner in the Globex contest. I've joined the photography club at school. They've got a darkroom with five enlargers, and the other kids are great about explaining stuff to me. By the way, there's something I've been meaning to ask you. I know that Greg gave you my diary down at P.B. So now that you know my life story, what do you think of it?

Love,
Samantha

I reread it once, sealed it, and mailed it before I could change my mind.

Of course, I was a wreck waiting for an answer, but all I got was a frustrating little note five days later that said:

Samantha,

See you at the awards dinner. We'll talk then.

Keith

My heart did flip-flops as I read his note. Was the awards dinner coming up soon? Dad hadn't said a word.

I paced my room until I heard a car pull into the driveway, then I dashed downstairs.

"Dad," I demanded, barely saying hello, "when's the awards dinner for the Saint Martin trip?"

"Saturday night," he told me. "You know, I've been so busy at the office that I completely forgot to mention it. Did you want to go?"

"Yes," I answered emphatically. Then I confessed that I had entered photographs in the competition.

"Why didn't you tell me before?"

"For my own pride. I wanted to keep my entries as separate from you as I could."

"That's silly," he said. "But what's done is done. Anyway, I understand we were beseiged with entries, and the judges are having a very hard time deciding on the winners."

"But will I be able to go to the dinner? I'm not expecting to win anything, but I'd love to see the pictures and find out who gets to be the big winner."

"I can understand that," he told me. "And I'd be just delighted to have you join your mother and me. Samantha, I'd love to see the photographs you took at Paradise Bay. Have you got anything to show me?"

I ran upstairs to get my contact sheets, and I nervously showed them to Dad. He looked through them slowly without saying a word.

"Good for you, Samantha," he said finally, giving me a big smile. "Some of these are excellent. I knew Keith Garson would be the right teacher."

All this happened on Wednesday night, which meant I had exactly three days to prepare myself for seeing Keith. You can imagine what a state I was in. There was nothing in the world I wanted more than to see him. But—what would happen between us? It was a minor miracle that I made it through school without walking into a wall or making a fool of myself in class. By Saturday evening my nervousness was really obvious.

Dad seemed to think I was hung up on winning a prize. "Please remember," he kept saying, "you only just started taking pictures."

"Just having entered is prize enough for me," I assured him. "After all, I'd never even held a camera before our trip to Paradise Bay."

"I'm proud of you, Samantha," he told me with a little more enthusiasm than seemed necessary.

Mom, on the other hand, must have had a clearer picture of what was going on. For one thing, it would have been pretty hard for her to ignore the five rejected outfits piled up on my bedroom chair while I was getting dressed on Saturday. In the end I chose a full, pleated green skirt, a white blouse, and dressy, low-heeled pumps. All very comfortable but fashionable.

Greg, of course, was dying to go to the dinner, but Mom had the good sense to make him stay home with a baby-sitter. I loved saying goodbye to him as we went out to the car. He was really angry to be left behind, but I figured that was his punishment for his nasty trick at Paradise Bay.

As we drove along the Long Island Expressway, Dad revealed that he did, in fact, now know the names of the winners, but he refused to reveal anything more. "It's not my place to say," he explained as the brilliant lights of New York's skyline came into view. "You'll have to wait just a bit longer. But I will tell you that the exhibit is hanging in the office gallery, and it looks just great. And a delicious French dinner is going to be served in the executive dining room."

Dad drove through the hectic city streets and into the parking lot under the office building that housed Globex headquarters. I was getting more and more tense every moment. After all, this time I was going to see Keith, and we were finally going to talk openly and honestly. Was this the beginning or the end?

Chapter Fifteen

As we stood in the elevator going up to the twenty-fourth floor, I took deep, slow breaths. I was making too big a deal out of seeing Keith, I warned myself. He was probably not even focused on seeing me. It didn't take much to realize that the biggest thing on his mind at that moment was winning a prize.

The doors of the elevator opened on to the plushly carpeted hallway and glass doors of the Globex reception area. Dad led us through a separate set of doors into the gallery. The perfect white walls were hung with a mixture of color as well as black-and-white photographs, all individually mounted behind glass.

"It's a large show," Mom commented. "I had no idea so many Globex people were actually photographers themselves."

"It speaks well for our people and our trip," Dad said. "The prize-winning shots are on the front panel over there, and the other entries fill the rest of the gallery." He directed us to where the winners were and stood by as we studied the prints.

"That's Keith's photograph!" I exclaimed as I stared at a beautiful black-and-white shot of the fish seller at the Marigot market. "Mom, Dad, Keith's won first prize! Oh, that's so wonderful!" I cried, my enthusiasm bubbling over.

"Yes," agreed Dad, "and you should have seen the look on Dave's face yesterday when he found out. He was practically the proudest father I've ever seen."

"And well he should be," Mom said.

"Now take a look at the second and third prize winners, too," Dad directed. "Because they're also excellent, and don't, by any means, ignore the honorable mention category. Some wonderful photos are there, especially in my book."

I couldn't imagine why he was making such a big deal about the other entries until a familiar black-and-white photograph of a heron standing in a pond caught my eye. "Dad, that's my picture," I blurted out. "I can't believe it. I won an honorable mention!"

"Yes, you did. As proud fathers go, I'm right up there with Dave Garson. And I know you're proud, too."

"Am I ever!"

"Samantha, this picture is really impressive," Mom said seriously. She broke into a huge smile and hugged me. "And congratulations on winning."

Dad had to run off to take care of business, and Mom said she'd give him a hand. "First," she said, "I'm going to check my hair in the ladies' room. Want to come, Samantha?"

"No, thanks. I'll see you later."

What I really wanted was to be alone with the photographs and my memories of Saint Martin. I wanted to think about the good times once more and ignore the bad. And that's exactly what I did as I walked from picture to picture. Lost in fantasy, I hardly noticed the people who were beginning to fill up the gallery. I even forgot my nervousness about seeing Keith, until I felt someone tap me on the shoulder. I turned around, and suddenly we were face to face.

"Samantha, I found you," he said, his voice filled with excitement and relief. "I thought I never would in this crowd."

He looked handsome in a white shirt with a beige crew neck and a navy blazer over it. Even with his tan nearly faded, he looked as gorgeous as ever. All I wanted to do was throw myself in his arms. He was grinning from ear to ear, and I thought for a moment that he wanted to do exactly the same thing. But neither of us made a move, and the moment soon passed.

"Keith, congratulations on winning first prize," I said.

"Thanks a lot. I can't tell you how great I feel."

"And Dad said your father was really proud of you."

"Yes," he agreed, still beaming. "This is going to mean a lot to me when I have to make my college decision."

"I'm glad for you," I told him.

"And, Samantha, let's not forget your photograph. It looks great, and an honorable mention for a beginner is really something."

"I'm completely surprised," I admitted.

"I'm not. You worked very hard."

"I did," I agreed. "But I never expected to win anything."

"Are you still going strong?" he asked.

"Yes," I assured him.

Pretty soon we were in the middle of a conversation about photography, talking as if we had never been parted. The party went on around us, but we hardly noticed. Of course, Keith's father interrupted us a few hundred times to introduce yet another business associate to his prize-winning son. Eventually everyone headed upstairs for dinner, except Keith and me.

"Alone at last!" he said jokingly as the remaining guests disappeared into the elevator. Pulling me into his arms, he gave me a warm and gentle kiss. I closed my eyes and kissed him back. It was paradise revisited.

I nearly let myself get lost in our kiss, but my conscience said no, and I pulled away. I had to settle a few things first. "Keith, I have to talk to you right now!"

"And what have we been doing for the last hour?" he said, laughing.

"No, I have to talk to you about something awful. About my diary."

"What about it?"

"Well, since you read it you must know how I always wanted to apologize to you for what I did in Montauk. In Saint Martin, when I got to like you so much, I got even more embarrassed about it, so embarrassed that I couldn't tell you how I really felt."

"No, I didn't know that," he said calmly but with interest.

"What do you mean?"

"I never read your diary. Didn't Greg tell you? When I gave it back, I told him I refused to read it. I chewed his ear off about invading your privacy and stuff like that."

"He never said a word!"

"He was pretty embarrassed himself, let me tell you," Keith said.

"You never read all the stuff I said about you—" The truth was beginning to sink in, and I stopped before I said too much.

"No, never," he told me with a grin, "but I'd be glad to hear it now."

"Well, then," I said, "would you please accept my apologies for the way I acted way back in Montauk. I always meant to say I was sorry."

"Samantha, that was ancient history. I forgave you ages ago."

"You did?"

"Yes, and then I fell for you all over again in Saint Martin."

"But you never told me!"

"Well, I certainly didn't want to get burned again," he said. "OK, let me set the record straight here. I have to admit that I was really hurt back there in Montauk, but I didn't think about it again until our Saint Martin trip. When your father asked about photography lessons, I was definitely uneasy. For one thing, I was afraid I still cared about you, and I didn't know what to do about it. So each time we had our lessons I went into hiding."

"So I noticed."

"If Paul hadn't been there, I never could have done it."

"And I kept wishing you would invite me sometimes."

"I wanted to, but I was still afraid."

"Afraid, of me! I can't believe it!"

"Believe it."

"Well, it's sure not easy to get you to talk about your feelings. And as for letter writing, you're even worse!" I complained.

"What's wrong with my letters?"

"They're so newsy—and impersonal."

"Do you care?" he asked softly.

"Of course I do. Can't you tell!"

"Then I guess I have to break down and confess what I've been feeling for weeks. You're really special to me, Samantha. I guess it's safe to admit it now that there's no hotel room for you to hide in."

"Oh, Keith." I laughed as he took me gently by the shoulders and kissed me again.

"Do you think anyone would notice if we didn't show up for dinner?" he murmured.

"No. Just your parents, my parents, and a couple hundred other people. You're the number-one photographer around here."

"What timing," he complained.

I'm not sure if either of us ate any of the gourmet dinner Globex served us. We were too intent on each other. And when the evening was over, I floated home, happier than I'd ever been before in my life. Keith and I were going to see a lot of each other on weekends, we had decided. In between, we would take lots of pictures, talk on the phone, and write letters.

A few days later, when that first written message arrived, cheerful and newsy as it was, I couldn't take my eyes off the closing words. Neatly and boldly he had finally written, "Love, Keith."